TOO HOT!

AVERY GILES

RIPTIDE
PUBLISHING

TOO HOT!

AVERY GILES

RIPTIDE
PUBLISHING

Riptide Publishing
PO Box 1537
Burnsville, NC 28714
www.riptidepublishing.com

Too Hot!

Cover art: Natasha Snow, natashasnowdesigns.com
Editors: Carole-ann Galloway, Veronica Vega, May Peterson
Layout: L.C. Chase, lcchase.com/design.htm

ISBN: 978-1-62649-860-0

First edition
October, 2018

Also available in ebook:
ISBN: 978-1-62649-848-8

TABLE OF
CONTENTS

CHAPTER 1

Eli scowled at Pistol, his glare unwavering. "There's no point in lying to me. I know what you did. Admit it. You're a scheming, cold-hearted murderer."

A loaded pause passed.

Pistol blinked slowly at him before flicking his tail twice and sashaying to the side, revealing the body of the dead mouse he'd been hiding behind his rotund haunches.

"I knew it. Fucking cats."

Sighing, Eli stood for a moment in the middle of his kitchen, the white tile warming beneath his bare feet. Gray light filtered through the tattered blinds, a precursor to dawn. It was too damn early for this.

He grabbed a paper towel off the roll by the sink, carefully scooped up the poor mouse's body, and dumped it in the trash. Then he tied the drawstrings on the half-full bag and carried it outside, shivering as the cool morning air sliced through his tank top and shorts.

Wasting a bag was a shame, but he couldn't have a corpse stinking up his little kitchen, and there was always a chance Pistol would knock over the trash to collect his prize as soon as Eli left for work.

Once more, with venom, he muttered, "Fucking cats," as he tossed the garbage into the can.

When he turned back to the little house, his eyes skimmed over familiar details: faded paint, overgrown hedges, and a lawn that needed cutting. It was hard to find the energy to maintain it on the best of days, especially considering he rented. The darkened kitchen window reflected the outline of his tall form back to him, but no detail.

The reflection was broken, as if a stone had been launched into a pond, when two fuzzy heads appeared in the holes in the blinds. Eli had stopped bothering to replace the covers. The cats would just tear them up again regardless.

Walking back inside, he clicked his tongue at the two animals. "Moxie, Chutzpah. Down."

They stared at him. Moxie, the green-eyed tabby, obeyed only to attack the all-black blob on the floor that was Pistol. As she gnawed on his ear, he glanced dolefully up at Eli.

"Don't look at me." Eli shrugged. "Fight back if you want her to stop."

Pistol rolled over in response, exposing his large stomach. Chutzpah turned back to the window, as if Moxie's compliance counted toward his own as well.

"Get a cat, they said." Eli sat at the small wooden table next to the fridge. The smell of brewing coffee filled his nose in the most pleasurable way. "It'll be fun, they said. Oh, but you can't stop at one. They need a friend! And when a stray ginger boy shows up at your door, shivering and starving, it's not like you can turn him away. I swear, every month I go without a boyfriend, I earn another cat. Like some sort of loneliness Boy Scout badge."

Chutzpah twisted around to look at him, orange eyes seeming to say, *Talking to us is not helping your case.*

Thankfully, the coffee maker chirped just then. He poured himself a cup and splashed in some milk, enough to lighten the color a shade or two.

As it did every day, his mother's voice echoed in his head, *"You like your coffee the same color as your eyes—"* "He tore open two Splenda packets and added them as well. *"—and as sweet as your heart."*

The memory wrenched his mouth out of the frown it'd been stuck in since his alarm had gone off. His smile widened when he glanced up and caught sight of a cluster of photos stuck to the fridge with colorful magnets. His mother, Delilah Johnson, saluted him, all decked out in her blue Air Force uniform, the triangular hat almost lost in her voluminous hair.

Eyes suddenly stinging, he glanced away and made a mental note to call his dad after work. See how he was doing. It was hard to believe eight years had passed. He still found it hard to look at her dark eyes, shining with life.

"Gonna make you proud today, Mom." He gulped down his too-hot coffee and dumped the dregs into the sink. "Or at least, I'm gonna do my best."

He slipped through the spartan living room to his bedroom. More photos of family members littered his nightstand and bureau. From his closet, he produced one of his many blue Louisville Fire Department T-shirts and standard-issue khaki pants.

The dry season had been over for months, and a wet spring had settled over most of Kentucky. If he wanted to, he could show up in civvies—he probably wasn't going to do much more than cook, clean, and work out—but if he did, and they got a call, everyone would blame him. People who thought the theater was superstitious had clearly never been to a fire station.

If Mom were here, she would have teased him. She'd never believed in things like bad luck or jinxes. Her philosophy had always been simple: you got back what you put out, nothing more and nothing less. Unlike Eli's father, who hobbled down to church every Sunday and prayed for everything from good poker hands to winning the lottery.

I miss her so much.

He sat on the neatly made bed to pull on his socks and boots, losing himself in the routine. When he was finished, he ducked into the bathroom to brush his teeth, taking a long look at himself in the mirror. The bags under his eyes were darker than his brown skin, almost like bruises. His hair fell in springy curls over his brow.

His shirt needed to be ironed, but he didn't have time for that before work. He smoothed out whatever wrinkles he could see with his hands. He cut an impressive figure in his uniform, but the muscle wasn't for show. If he had to lift a smoldering beam off someone, he had to do it fast.

After grabbing his things and an apple for the road, he searched for his cats so he could say goodbye. Chutzpah was still in the window, Moxie had joined him again, and Pistol was splayed out in front of the fridge like a puddle of ink. "Be good, y'all. Guard the house while I'm gone. And *please*, no more mice?"

They didn't respond—thank God. All he needed was to start hallucinating his cats were talking to him. He left through the front door, letting the screen bang shut behind him. Outside, wet grass made slick sounds beneath his boots.

The sky was slate gray and opaque. The only indication that a sunrise was currently happening was the gradual lightening of the thick charcoal clouds. Maybe he could convince Chief Sappenfield to let them leave the trucks out for a nice soak. It'd beat washing them for the third time this week.

A nondescript green sedan waited for him in the cracked driveway. He waved to Mrs. Kavanagh—the little old white lady next door he was extra careful to be sweet to, even though she always eyed him like he was going to snatch her pocketbook—and climbed in. The engine sprang to life the second he turned the key, not with an impressive roar but with a reliable, midrange purr.

As Louisville slid past outside the windows, Eli's eyes roved over buildings he'd seen so many times, he barely registered them anymore. The neighborhood market. Strings of cute mom-and-pop shops. The elementary school he quietly resented because if he drove past it around three, the speed limit changed to fifteen miles per hour. All of it was crowned by the small but stately skyline in the distance. A dozen or so skyscrapers cut the metallic sky into a jigsaw puzzle. It was no New York City, but it suited Eli fine.

His fire station—one of many in the metro area—had become a second home to him in the past five years. To be honest, it was a big-ass glorified garage where the trucks slept when they weren't in use, but his heart still fluttered when he caught sight of the proud redbrick façade, wedged in the heart of downtown between a plain building and a filling station where the FD, PD, and EMS all fueled their trucks. He pulled into the parking lot next to the firehouse. Within seconds, a young black woman appeared as if by magic.

"Eli!" Anette, the FD's newest recruit, jogged over to his car, her wild hair barely contained by the firefighter's helmet jammed onto her head. Eli would bet money she and Thorogood had been racing to see who could get their gear on fastest again.

She flashed perfect white teeth at him. "Right on time, as per usual."

Eli locked his car and smiled. "Hey, Anette. You're awfully peppy for this ungodly hour."

"Gotta be to balance out Chief Sappenfield."

"Ah. I take it she's in one of her sunny moods?"

"About as sunny as this weather." Anette frowned up at the sky, her dark eyes narrowing with disapproval. "Think it'll rain?"

"According to the forecast, it's guaranteed. I'm calling it right now: we're in for a quiet morning."

Anette laughed. "You know you just jinxed us, right?"

"*You* know I don't believe in that crap."

Not really, anyway.

She led the way to the station, chattering all the while about this and that: what she'd done over the weekend, a joke McPherson had told her, and date night with her new boyfriend. Her energy seeped into Eli as if by osmosis, perking him up. By the time they walked into the station, he finally felt ready for the day.

The familiar smell of diesel and rubber hit him full force. Was it sad he'd grown to love that smell? A cherry-red fire truck gleamed under the overhead lights. Decades ago, the first truck had been named Dottie, and the tradition lived on. Currently, they were on Dottie III. It was filthy, which meant it'd need to be cleaned. Again. That was one stereotype about firefighters that Eli couldn't deny: they were constantly washing their dirt-magnet trucks.

Hanging around the truck were three other members of the first crew: McPherson, Rogers, and Thorogood. They were decent guys, and great at their jobs, but Eli hadn't warmed to any of them. They were older, white, and conservative, for the most part. Like the majority of Louisville.

Only Anette had gone out of her way to be friendly. He suspected that was partially because the others treated her with similar reserve, for similar reasons. It could also be a bit of a self-fulfilling prophecy. Folks at the station had assumed he and Anette were friends long before they'd actually connected. Anette joked that it was because they were the youngest, or the hottest, or had the most swag. But they both knew the real reason.

"Johnson, get in here." Chief Sappenfield's barking voice sounded from the glassed-in dispatch room on the far end of the station, opposite the lockers where they stowed their gear and the proverbial firefighter's pole that spat them out onto the ground level.

"Uh-oh," Anette whispered. "She sounds crankier than before."

Eli hustled over to the office. "Ma'am."

Chief Sappenfield was standing straight-backed between the dispatch radio and the charging station where the individual radios for the first and second crew were all nestled together. Her back was to him, but when he entered the office, she twisted around.

He assessed her quickly, searching for signs that he was in for a verbal beatdown. Tall, Latina, mid-forties, with a semipermanent scowl on her face. She didn't appear any more agitated than usual, however, so perhaps everything was fine.

Anette's "cranky" description had been fair, and much nicer than the "hard-ass" moniker the chief had earned from the others, but Eli had never known the battalion chief to be anything other than reasonable. She demanded what she knew you could give. If you fell short of her expectations, her disapproval would be nothing compared to your disappointment in yourself.

"Good morning, Johnson," she said briskly, getting the pleasantry over with.

"Morning, Chief. You asked to see me?"

"I wanted to give you a heads-up. I changed the schedule in the rec room. Rogers has to take his daughter to an early doctor's appointment. You got the evening shift on Friday."

Eli only barely suppressed a groan. "Evening" shifts for them were more like graveyard shifts. Someone had to be here around the clock in case a call came in, rainy season or not. As the only person in the first crew with no children, Eli often got stuck filling schedule holes. It was absolute *murder* on his social life.

Another Friday evening spent here, alone. Well, at least I'll have the rec room to myself. Might actually get a turn at the Xbox for once.

Nodding, Eli smiled. "Fine by me. Hope Rogers's daughter is all right." His gaze drifted to the arm of the chief's decorated uniform. Words jumped out at him from the embroidered badge near her shoulder: *Honor. Courage. Duty. Dedication.* The motto of their department. Words his mother would have taken very seriously. Words he tried to live by.

"Something on your mind?" Chief Sappenfield asked.

Eli toyed with a couple of lies before discarding them. He'd never been any good at lying, and the chief had more than earned honesty from him. "Been thinking about my mom a lot today for some reason."

Instantly, Chief Sappenfield's hard eyes melted. She patted him on the arm. "It never really goes away, does it? Grief, I mean. Don't tell the guys, but I still have dreams where I talk to my father. Waking up is bittersweet."

"My lips are sealed. Thanks, Chief. I'll check out the schedule and then get to work."

"Good. Lord only knows there's always something to do around here." The dispatch radio behind her buzzed right on cue. A gruff male voice barked the chief's name. She gestured at Eli as she picked it up. "Dismissed."

Scuttling away, Eli made a pit stop at the rows of tall metal lockers. They each had their own, and they were mostly full of everyone's turnout gear: fireproof jackets, pants, suspenders, breathing masks, and more.

Almost everyone, however, also kept photos of their families taped inside. Smiling wives, kids holding puppies, that sort of thing. Eli was the exception, having no spouse to display. Even Anette had one of those cheesy photo booth strips of her and her latest squeeze.

Maybe you should propose to the Xbox and call it a day.

After checking his gear, Eli headed for the back of the bay. It housed the master air tanks that filled their individual ones. He'd serviced his tank only yesterday, but he checked it regardless. Not that he'd jinxed them or anything.

Next, he trekked upstairs to the communal areas. There was the rec room—where they spent hours of downtime huddled together on old, squishy couches—followed by the kitchen, where they took turns cooking for everyone during long shifts.

To the right was a storeroom with extra equipment and cots for grabbing power naps. It was the neatest storeroom in existence, because it also housed the fire pole. The way to it was kept clear at all times, on pain of having Chief Sappenfield flay you alive. Finally, behind an imposing wooden door, lay the chief's office, a place they all dreaded. The chief only ever called someone in there if they *really* fucked up.

In the rec room, a whiteboard displayed the chores rotation and the schedule—who was on duty, who was at home, and who could be called for backup. Eli was almost always in the first crew, since his schedule was flexible. The second crew only got called for big fires or if a second fire broke out in their jurisdiction at the same time.

Sure enough, Eli was working three night shifts this week, only two of which he'd signed up for. This was what he got for complaining about having to wake up at the crack of dawn. The universe was always listening, and it loved to make him eat his words.

Much as he groused, working nights wasn't terrible. The station was a different place when it wasn't buzzing with people. A little spooky, sure, but the sight of Dottie III and the gleam of the fire pole always put him at ease. Eli had done some of his best thinking while stretched out on a cot, one ear tuned to the alarm that could go off at any moment and his brain a million miles away.

There was no denying it was lonely, however. At twenty-eight, he was far from old, but every Friday he spent with only himself for company was starting to feel more and more like a missed opportunity. His mom had always told him to focus on his education, and then later on his career. She'd said everything else would fall into place when it was ready.

Well, he had a career he loved, and he was settled. Where was the rest? When were things going to fall into place for him?

He hadn't expected an answer, but in a sense, he got one.

The alarm tripped, blaring through the station with such force it drowned out thought. Eli's instincts took over. He was out of the rec room and into storage in seconds, where the fire pole jutted up out of the floor to the ceiling. His muscles knew precisely what to do as he grabbed it, wrapped his ankles around it, and slid smoothly down.

The garage was an upturned anthill. Through the glass, he spotted Chief Sappenfield on the dispatch radio. Only one alarm had tripped, indicating a small fire, but judging by the grave look on her face, something was wrong.

Eli didn't waste time trying to read her. He scrambled to the lockers along with the rest of his squad: McPherson, Rogers, and Anette. His heart pumped gasoline and broken glass. It was an incredible high: the mix of adrenaline, fear, and raw determination that flooded through him.

Moments like this made him feel unstoppable. Strong. Like he could rip the door of his locker clean off the hinges. But it also made him feel acutely vulnerable. One wrong move, and it could all be over. People could get hurt. Or worse.

Out of the corner of his eye, Eli saw Thorogood, the lead on the run crew, on his radio, repeating back the information from emergency dispatch. God forbid they wasted precious time driving to the wrong location. The faster they got to the scene, the more likely they could contain the fire before it spread.

This was where endless training and drills came into play. They had a little over two minutes to get their gear on and load into the truck. Every time that alarm went off, Eli was suddenly traveling through Jell-O. His limbs moved in slow motion as he pulled on his gear, assembled the pieces of his mask, and jammed his helmet onto his head.

Despite this, according to his internal count, he was dressed and ready in a minute and ten seconds: his personal best. McPherson, the resident veteran, had already finished and was readying Dottie III. Eli ran to help him. The water tanks would have been filled already, but he checked the gauges anyway. Full. Same for gas. Same for the spare air tanks. They were good to go.

Anette and Rogers appeared, geared up, followed by Thorogood.

He shoved radios into their hands. "There's a confirmed fire at Woodrow Elementary."

Holy shit, a school. No wonder the chief had looked perturbed.

"Students have been evacuated. The chief says to move your asses. We're not taking any chances with this one. I'll dispatch the second crew ASAP. Tune to channel one-seven-five."

They didn't pause to do more than grunt confirmation before they piled into the truck: two in the front, two in the back. Eli scrambled into the passenger seat next to Rogers, but in his head, he was already at the scene. All fires were frightening, but one at a school carried an extra level of trepidation. The tension in the air was thick as steel wool.

That's the same school I'm always complaining about. Fuck. I'll never do that again. Maybe I really did jinx us.

When they were all belted in, and the others had indicated via radio that they were ready, Eli flipped a switch on the dash. The siren blared to life as the white and red lights started flashing. Visibility was always paramount, but with children on the line, they were going to be barreling through every red light they came across.

While Rogers navigated the multiton vehicle out onto the street—cars skittering out of the way like mice—Eli tuned their dash radio to the correct frequency. Even over the siren, he could hear the dispatchers talking.

". . . police and EMS have arrived on the scene. Over."

"The fire appears to have started in the gym and is spreading quickly. Over."

"Head counts of the children are being conducted, and it seems not all are accounted for. Police are attempting to clear pedestrians from the area and set up barricades. Over."

Voices ricocheted off each other as news poured in. Eli's blood sang with exhilaration, and nerves plucked taut strings in his stomach.

They saw the smoke long before the small elementary school came into view. The scene they arrived on was undiluted chaos, a life-sized hornet's nest. Children and teachers were huddled together on the green front lawn while a white cinderblock building smoldered a dozen yards away.

Ambulances and police cars ringed the school like a moat. Paramedics were checking several children with ash-smudged faces, and police were fighting to set up a barrier. Literally fighting, because a dozen or so civilians—teachers?—were trying to sprint toward the gym. Eli got it, he really did, but hysteria would do more harm than good.

As they pulled up, he assessed the gym for entry points, potential danger, and the likeliest origin of the flames. It was practically instinct to him now as his eyes ticked off the scorched left side and intact glass windows. The building itself was mostly cement, which had undoubtedly stymied the spread of the fire. It hadn't reached the main school building yet, and since they were separate, it likely wouldn't.

It looked as though an equipment shed next to the gym had been the origin point, and the flames had spread via dead grass to a side door before creeping inside. If the gym had a wooden basketball court, it would certainly burn. Things could get much, much worse.

But the filmy smoke and lack of visible flames suggested they'd gotten here before too much damage had been done. There was hope.

Rogers parked the truck next to the closest fire hydrant and slammed on the brakes. Eli lurched forward, his seat belt digging into his chest. If it hurt, he was numb to it.

McPherson's voice barked over their radios. "Goddamn it, Rogers. You drive like a fifteen-year-old with a learner's permit and a dream. Over."

Rogers yanked his radio off his belt and held it to his mouth. "Bite me. Over."

Eli kicked open his door and jumped down to the ground, landing lightly on the balls of his feet. The thick, acrid smell of smoke burned his nostrils. Anette and McPherson burst out of the back of the truck, grabbed the hose, and hooked it up to the hydrant with practiced ease.

Rogers cut the siren before exiting the truck as well. "Marshall. McPherson. You're on the hose. Keep the flames from spreading to the main building. Johnson, you're with me. We're heading in to search for missing children and assess the interior damage. According to dispatch, the current head count says two kids are unaccounted for."

"Got it," they all said in unison.

Crouching low, Rogers led the way to the gym at a light sprint. Eli followed, flipping his mask down onto his face, securing it, and enabling the air flow. They needed to be fast. Any children who might be inside were currently filling their tiny lungs with smoke. It'd cause them serious damage in a quarter of the time it would take for an adult. It was protocol to escort victims from the building *before* giving them air, but fuck that. If Eli found a kid, his mask was coming off. He would survive.

As it turned out, that wouldn't be necessary.

Rogers had just reached the double doors leading into the gym and was preparing to force the metal open with gloved hands—or an ax, failing that—when the doors shuddered.

"Get back," Rogers yelled, voice muffled by his own mask. "The heat must be pressurizing. It's going to blow."

"We should—"

Eli never got to finish that sentence.

The doors burst open. Eli braced himself for an explosion—thoughts scattering like feathers as a fresh wave of panic swept through him—but it never came. Instead, two figures emerged: a pair of adults who each had a child cradled in their arms.

On instinct, Eli ran for the nearest one, a young white man with a soot-streaked face. He was carrying a sobbing girl who couldn't have been more than six. Her tears tracked clean paths down her dirty face.

Eli opened his mouth to ask if they were hurt, but before he could, the man caught sight of him and smiled, bright and easy. Eli couldn't pinpoint what it was, but something about the man's relaxed demeanor stopped him in his tracks.

"My hero," the man said. "Perfect timing."

Well, that was a new one. Most people Eli met in front of burning buildings were terrified, but this one was cracking jokes. Eli scrutinized him, flummoxed. The man had the deepest brown eyes Eli had ever seen, dark like coal. They drew Eli in so much he nearly took an involuntary step forward. The man was tall too. And built. Was he a teacher? The gym instructor, judging by his body.

What the fuck? Eli mentally slapped himself. *This is an emergency. Focus.*

He cleared his throat. "Are you hurt? Is anyone else in there?"

The man shook his head, dispelling ash from brunet hair. "We're fine. These two were the only ones left. We found them huddled under the bleachers. Everyone else evacuated. The fire is contained to an equipment room for now, but I doubt it'll stay that way for long."

In the most eloquent moment of his life, Eli said, "Uh . . . wow."

The guy smiled again in response, and it was the perfect mixture of cocky and coy. When their eyes met, even through the smoke and Eli's mask, it was like one of the tongues of flame licked up Eli's spine.

Rogers interrupted their pseudo moment. "I'll double-check for stragglers. Johnson, get the civilians to the EMS, then radio the others and tell them where to concentrate the hose. If the fire hasn't spread too far, we might be able to contain it with our extinguishers."

"Yes, sir."

Behind them, a loud gushing sound indicated that Anette and McPherson were in position and had started the hose. Spray hit the back of Eli's neck as pressurized water descended onto the side of the gym feet from them.

Eli radioed in the info and waved for the survivors to follow him, including a wailing boy and a young woman in a cardigan who perfectly fit Eli's mental image of a librarian. He made a beeline for the nearest ambulance. Paramedics rushed forward to examine the children and the woman, who relayed the whole story at double speed. The man, however, handed over the girl and then hung back, his expression pinched.

Curiosity poked at Eli, but he couldn't very well stop what he was doing and ask the mystery man what was on his mind. As soon as the civilians were in the hands of paramedics, he sprinted back to the gym.

Inside, rows of compact bleachers lined a large wooden basketball court. The air shimmered from the flames that were licking their way out of an open side door. Most people would never know what real heat felt like. It was powerful. It had density, similar to getting smacked full force by an ocean wave.

A dull roar buffeted Eli's ears, like the snarl of a distant beast. Only this beast was right in front of him. It didn't matter how many times he came face-to-face with a fire, it never failed to make fear slither down his spine and pool in his gut.

Fighting a primal instinct to flee, he ran to Rogers's side. Rogers had readied one of the canisters of compressed water they all carried with them and was beating back the fire. Juvenile wisps of flame were all they were up against, despite what Eli's clenching gut was screaming at him. He grabbed his extinguisher and joined Rogers.

Between their efforts and the hose outside, the fire took twenty minutes to tame. There were a few harrowing moments where the smoke got so thick it obscured Eli's vision—making his pulse rattle in his ears—but beyond that, it went as well as could be expected.

After, he surveyed the smoldering remains with a leaden stomach. Even small fires caused frightening amounts of damage. Thank God the actual school hadn't been touched. The faces of the two frightened children popped into Eli's head, followed by another smiling face he could picture with too-perfect clarity.

He turned to Rogers, who was kicking a smoldering beam to see if any lingering sparks flew up. "Sir, with your permission, I'm going to tell Marshall and McPherson to cut the hose. Then I'll rendezvous with the police and see if the forensic team is here." *And if I happen to stop by the ambulances and check on the civilians while I'm at it, then I'm simply being thorough.*

"Go ahead." Rogers waved him off. "Looks like there's nothing left to see here. Although, be a dear: if you hear a blood-curdling scream, feel free to mosey on back."

With a snort, Eli headed out of the gym at a light jog. As soon as he was far enough away, he turned back and surveyed the exterior damage. Where flames had once licked along the ground, there was now ash and soot. The shed had collapsed, but the gym looked more or less fine, minus a blown-out side door and some scorch marks.

As promised, he stopped by Anette and McPherson first and declared the all clear over the deafening roar of the water. They cut the hose and began the process of packing it back up. It was a two-person job, so Eli headed for the nearest cop car. The officer there informed him that forensics were on their way.

While they swapped information about the fire, Eli's eyes drifted over the officer's shoulder to the ambulance where he'd left the two adults and children. The librarian-looking woman was more or less where Eli had last seen her, but the kids and the man weren't in sight.

Disappointment gurgled in Eli's stomach. *You were hoping to see him again.* He internally scolded himself and was about to return his attention to the officer when movement caught his eye. It was the man. He wasn't gone after all, just edging toward the crowd's periphery with his head down like he didn't want to be seen.

Holy shit, it almost worked too. Funny that he can blend in so easily when he stuck out so much to me before. Is he trying to leave the scene before being interviewed?

Eli interrupted the officer midsentence. "Will you excuse me for a moment? I want to ask one of the civs some questions."

"Sure thing." The officer stepped back. "When you're finished, send them my way. Detective Thorpe wants statements while the events are still fresh in everyone's minds."

"Will do."

Eli headed for the ambulances, eyes on his prize. As he watched, the man edged farther away from the buzzing crowds, slow and steady. It really seemed like he was preparing to make a break for it. Shock had probably set in, overriding his better judgment.

Not on my watch.

"Hey!" Eli broke into a jog. "Did the paramedics release you?"

The man jerked his head toward him, eyes wide. A second later, a familiar grin slipped onto his handsome face. "Hero. Fancy seeing you again."

"That's not my name, and you didn't answer my question." Eli eyed him, disabling his air flow and pulling his mask down so his voice was no longer muffled. "The paramedics will need to check you for injuries and smoke inhalation if they haven't already."

The man's grin warped into a grimace. "I'm not injured. Don't waste resources on me."

Eli stared at him. "Buddy, are you kidding? You escaped from a burning building. You need medical attention."

"I'm really fine." He was looking down at his shoes—well-worn red Converses. Was he shy? He hadn't seemed like it before when he was smiling and cracking jokes.

That's odd . . . ly intriguing.

"Are you afraid of needles or something? They're not going to give you an IV, I don't think." Eli was pushing past baffled and into curious now. It didn't hurt that when the man looked down, it made it apparent how long and dark his eyelashes were.

Stop thirsting. Damn. This is so not the time.

The man looked up, and somehow, that made it impossible for Eli to breathe. "I don't want the attention, is all." He nodded to the left.

Eli peered over. Camera crews had shown up, of course. Fucking vultures. The police were doing a good job of keeping the reporters from harassing the children, but that wasn't stopping them from trying. Four of them were pressed up against the orange barricades, recording devices in hand. The glee on their faces turned Eli's stomach.

Sighing, Eli glanced back. "I get what you're saying, but I'll be honest: attention is going to be tough to avoid." He wet his lips and asked a question that had been burning the tip of his tongue. "What's your name?"

"Charlie. Charlie Kinnear." The same cocksure smile from before slid slowly over Charlie's lips. "And you're Johnson?"

"How'd you— Oh, you heard Rogers earlier. Right. Eli Johnson." He took off one of his gloves and held out his hand. "Are you a teacher here?"

Charlie gave him a firm, warm shake that did things to Eli's stomach. "No, I was walking by and saw the flames. I heard children screaming, and then people came bursting out of the gym. I ran inside to see if anyone had gotten trapped or was hiding. I think the woman who also stayed behind to help is a teacher, though."

Eli was so distracted by the brush of Charlie's long fingers, it took him a moment to process that. "Wait a minute." A police officer tried to approach them, but Eli waved her off. "You did *what*?"

"I went in to look for stragglers. My nephew hides when he's scared, so I ducked under the bleachers, and—"

"Hold up." For a second time, Eli flat-out stared at him. "You saw flames, and ran *into* the building? Toward the danger? And you don't work here?"

"Uh, no?"

"Do you have a child who goes to school here?"

"No, I don't have any kids." Charlie frowned, and this time not even the pleasant shape of his mouth could distract Eli. "I know it wasn't the wisest move, but I was terrified. Instinct took over, and I did the first thing that came to mind."

"That's . . ." Eli struggled for the right words. "That's not how most people react to fear. Usually, they freeze or run away."

"Guess I'm wired wrong, then." He shuffled his feet. "I'm not in trouble, am I? I suppose I was trespassing. This is exactly why I don't want to talk to the police."

A long, silent moment passed—punctuated by sirens, frantic voices, and the din from the buzzing crowd—and then Eli pried his tongue from the roof of his mouth. "Charlie . . . you're not in trouble. You're a *hero*."

Charlie actually fell back a step. "What? No, I'm not. You're the hero. You do this every day."

Eli shook his head. "This is my job. I signed up for this. I don't deserve a medal for doing what I'm supposed to do. But you? You're a literal Good Samaritan. I mean, I have to pseudo lecture you and tell you to never, ever, *ever* do that again, but seriously, that's amazing. You should be getting interviewed by those reporters over there. 'Local Hero Dives into Fire and Saves Children.'"

"No!" Charlie quickly cleared his throat. "No. I *really* don't want any attention. I don't deserve it either. Anyone would have done the same thing. I'd like to get out of here before someone notices me."

Someone's already noticed you.

Eli couldn't claim to understand Charlie's aversion to the spotlight, but some people were like that. "You're going to have to give the police a statement. There's no way around that." He paused. "But I know some of the folks on the force pretty well. Worked a lot of arson cases with them. I'll see if I can call in a favor. Get you interviewed somewhere out of the public eye."

Charlie's smile was gorgeous. "Thank you, Eli."

"You're not off the hook medically, though. If you won't get checked out by the paramedics, I'm going to insist you let me give you some air. You're talking fine, so it seems like your lungs are okay, but there could be subtle damage. There's a lot of smoke out here, and there was more in the gym." Eli fixed on his sternest, professional-firefighter face. "This is nonnegotiable."

"I can live with that." In a move that took Eli completely by surprise, Charlie reached up and fingered the mask hanging by Eli's face. His knuckles skimmed Eli's jaw. "Are you taking me back to your truck, or can I use your mask? I'm not sure which option I find more appealing."

The flirtatious gleam in his eyes was unmistakable. Eli was grateful that blushes didn't usually show up on his brown skin, because he felt hot for reasons that had nothing to do with the fire.

"Um." He had to reboot his brain before he could convince his hands to move. Acting on rote muscle memory, he pulled off his helmet, dismantled his mask while keeping the hose attached, and handed it over. Then he enabled the air flow again. "Here you go. Steady breaths. Not too fast, or you'll get dizzy."

"Is this oxygen?"

"Oh God, no. Common misconception. Carrying an oxygen tank into a fire would be bad, on account of that whole combustion thing. This is compressed air. It's the same as what you're breathing right now, minus all the smoke."

"Interesting." Charlie held the mask to his face and breathed evenly. His eyes never left Eli as he did. "Be honest, how silly do I look?"

You don't look silly. You look . . . hot. Why is it turning me on to watch him using my equipment? Maybe it's like seeing a lover pull on one of your T-shirts. Jesus, I need to get back to work. Eventually, they're going to notice I'm missing.

That wasn't the only issue either. If Charlie was flirting with him—and Eli was fairly certain Charlie was—he couldn't flirt back. He was no stranger to people mistaking gratitude for romantic interest. He'd been reliably informed that his uniform didn't hurt either. Regardless, it was flat-out unethical to hit on someone in distress.

Still, with Charlie watching him with such blatant interest, it was hard to keep a grip on his errant thoughts.

After a minute, Charlie pulled the mask back. "Are you satisfied?"

That's a loaded question.

"Yeah, that's enough." Eli reached for his mask. "You pass."

"You're wrong, you know."

Eli blinked. "About what?"

"About you not being a hero. About you just doing your job. I don't buy that for a second."

Lips quirking up, Eli huffed. "Anyone ever tell you that you're stubborn?"

"Oh, yeah." Charlie stepped closer. "But I'm also told that's one of my charms." His gaze flickered briefly to Eli's mouth before he finally relinquished hold on the mask. "You know, I am a little short of breath, but I don't know if it's because of the smoke."

Eli's heart started pounding again for a whole new set of reasons. That . . . pretty much affirmed he was being flirted with. Words fell out of Eli's mouth before he could think them over. "What do you think it's from?"

Charlie's beautiful smile was back as he cocked his head and said, without hesitation, "You."

CHAPTER 2

C harlie had anticipated getting rejected. He wasn't usually the sort to come on strong, and his flirting skills were rusty to the point of causing tetanus. He'd figured securing a date with Eli the Hot Firefighter—fucking *swoon*—was a long shot.

Hell, if he'd gotten punched, it wouldn't have been that surprising. After all, he had no reason to believe Eli was into men, other than the way he kept staring deeply into Charlie's eyes. Charlie had always thought that was an expression, but Eli seemed to see *into* him. It was exhilarating. And a little intimidating.

What Charlie did not anticipate, however, was for Eli's handsome face to go hard as stone and for him to walk away without a word. Had Charlie fucked up somehow? Said the wrong thing? He found it hard to believe he'd misread the situation *that* badly.

He stared at Eli's back—which was broad and sculpted even under his heavy turnout coat—before tripping over himself running after him. Adrenaline was still hot in his veins, and he suspected he was a little high from smoke inhalation. Apparently, that translated to boldness. "Hey, wait!"

Eli didn't wait. Back still turned, he pulled a radio off his belt and asked someone named Marshall where he was needed.

Charlie paused until a woman's voice had stopped responding before he jogged up and grabbed Eli's arm. Holy hell. He felt corded muscles under his fingers and wondered about the rest of him. "Eli, what's wrong? Why are you leaving?"

"I have to get back to work." Eli's voice was firm but not unkind. He stopped walking, but he also studiously avoided looking at Charlie.

"I'm a firefighter, and there's a lot of work that still needs to be done. Reports that need to be filed, safety checks that need to be made. I have a team who's counting on me, Charlie."

Shit. I shouldn't be distracting him right now. I must seem so insensitive, hitting on someone at the scene of a crime involving children.

Even as guilt squeezed his lungs, Charlie couldn't seem to let Eli go, literally and figuratively. It was unusual for him to take one look at someone and know he wanted them. Something about Eli's manner drew Charlie in: his soothing way of speaking, and the confident set of his shoulders. Plus, he was handsome as all hell, and Charlie was positive he wasn't imagining the sparks flying between them.

Maybe don't bring up sparks.

Charlie tightened his grip on Eli's arm, though he swore he could feel how easy it would be for Eli to break away if he wanted. "I know this isn't ideal, and I swear, I'm not some heartless monster, but . . . let me buy you a coffee."

Eli's—large, gorgeous, hazelnut-brown—eyes widened. "Charlie. My guy. I couldn't be more on the job here."

"Not right now." Charlie shifted closer. "Another time. As a thank-you."

"You say that like I carried you out of the building or something. You were already on your way out when I arrived. What would you be thanking me for?"

Existing?

Somehow, he didn't think Eli would go for that answer. This was starting to get awkward, and Charlie should really take the hint, but . . . he didn't think he'd ever felt such instant chemistry with someone. They'd talked for all of ten minutes, and Charlie had already learned so much: Eli was funny, genuine, and had a protective streak that was off-the-charts endearing.

His presence was also like a soothing balm. The second Charlie had locked eyes with him outside of the gym, he'd somehow known he was going to be all right. Charlie didn't have a lot of certainties in life. Eli's steady bearing attracted Charlie almost as much as his looks. He wasn't the sort to do such impulsive things, so if his instincts were telling him to go for it, there had to be a reason.

He squared his shoulders. "Okay, I'll let you go. But hear me out: forget the thank-you." His voice was so firm, even he was surprised. "Have coffee with me because you want to. *If* you want to, that is."

Please say you do.

Eli sighed. "Let's cut to the chase. You're asking me out, right?"

Charlie swallowed. "Is that a bad thing?"

Eli was still for a moment. Then, his expression softened infinitesimally. Hope welled up in Charlie's chest.

"Look, Charlie, you seem nice and all, but—"

Those words stomped his hope flat.

"—I know what this is. You've probably never been in a situation like this before, right? A life-or-death one?"

Charlie didn't respond.

"I thought as much. Well, speaking from experience, adrenaline does funny things to people. This is far from the first time I've been hit on at the scene of a fire. Hell, I had a lady propose to me once."

A bark of laughter burst from Charlie, despite the misery blooming in his gut. "For real?"

"Oh yeah. She got down on one knee and everything. But don't worry, I let her down gently." He smiled, but his eyes were remorseful. "The point is, what you're feeling right now isn't real. The shock is going to wear off in a couple of hours, and you'll realize it was your pounding heart talking."

"That's not true. Well, the part about my heart is, but there's something here."

"How do you know?"

Charlie opened his mouth only to close it again and look down at his shoes, a habit of his that popped up whenever he was at a loss for words. Possibilities swirled around in his skull: *I've been so focused on work lately. I haven't been on a date in way too long. I thought it was because I was building my career, but the second I saw you . . .*

He couldn't say any of that out loud, though. Hell, it sounded weird in his own head. Eli was a complete stranger, connection or not. Charlie could very well be imagining this chemistry between them, and honestly, the longer he stayed here, the more likely it was someone would notice him. No amount of favors Eli pulled could save him then. Charlie had taken a chance and asked out a cute guy, he'd gotten shot down, and now he should move on. Like an adult.

Why then were his shoes still rooted to the ground?

"Give me a chance to prove you wrong."

Eli blinked at him, as if he honestly hadn't expected that response. "Huh?"

"Give me your number. I promise to wait at least twenty-four hours before calling you. If you never hear from me, then you were right, and I changed my mind as soon as all the excitement wore off." Charlie leaned in. "Or if you're flat-out not interested, you can tell me now, no excuses necessary. But if you feel what I'm feeling, then take a chance. It's win-neutral for you."

Blowing out a breath, Eli glanced between Charlie and the fire truck, as if he were considering making a run for it. "You really are stubborn, you know that?"

"Yeah." Charlie grinned. "Are you starting to find it charming?"

Eli searched his face. Charlie tried not to fidget under the scrutiny. Normally, he did his best to blend in, but the attention from Eli made his knees weak.

Before Eli could say anything more, there was a shout behind him. "Johnson!"

A pretty black woman in firefighter's gear identical to Eli's came jogging up. Her mask was also hanging around her neck, and she had a helmet tucked under her arm. "Are the two kids all right? And the people who saved them?"

"Uh," Eli sputtered. "Well—"

She glanced at Charlie, seeming to notice him for the first time. Her eyes traveled over his face—which he was sure was streaked with soot—and then between them. Charlie could almost see gears ticking behind her eyes as she undoubtedly took in how close to each other they were standing.

Charlie braced himself, but to his surprise, her face broke out into a grin. "Oh, I see how it is. Here I thought you gave us bad luck earlier. Turns out it was more like *fate*."

"Anette," Eli said, an edge of annoyance in his tone, "it's *not* what you're thinking."

"I'm not thinking anything." With a giggle, she patted Eli on the shoulder. "And I didn't see anything either. I'll tell Rogers you're busy checking on the children. That oughta buy you some time."

"We don't *need* time—"

But she was already jogging away, her giggles floating behind her like dandelion seeds.

Charlie bit his lip. "I didn't just get you in trouble, did I?"

"No." Eli sighed. "Anette's cool."

"What'd she mean by 'bad luck'?"

"Nothing really. Some firefighters are superstitious. Man, she is so going to corner me later and make me tell her everything."

"There's nothing to tell." Charlie paused for effect. "Yet."

Eli gave him a pointed look. "I *really* can't hit on a civilian. Like, pun fully intended, that's playing with fire."

"You're not hitting on me. I'm hitting on you. And I'm not a civilian, remember? I'm a hero." Charlie winked.

At that, Eli laughed, rich and deep. "All right, damn. I can't waste any more time debating with you. Gimme your phone."

Charlie almost fumbled it in his hurry to get it out of his pocket and into Eli's (large) waiting hand. A little voice in the back of his head told him Eli could be giving him a fake number right now. If Charlie was true to his word, he wouldn't know it until tomorrow.

If that's the case, then I'll know for sure I've been rejected. At least I can comfort myself with the knowledge that I gave it my best shot.

When Eli finished putting in his number, he handed Charlie's phone back and gave him the first real hint of hope in the form of a wide, bright smile. "It was nice meeting you, Charlie. If you start to feel dizzy or anything, go straight to a hospital."

Charlie opened his mouth to assure Eli he would, but he was interrupted by a loud beeping coming from his belt.

Eli snorted. "A pager? In this day and age? I thought only doctors and drug dealers still carried those."

"Who's to say I'm not a doctor?" Charlie teased.

"Or a drug dealer," Eli shot back.

Charlie side-stepped that comment and checked the page. Shit. He needed to make a phone call that he decidedly didn't want Eli to hear. "I have to get going."

"Sorry, but like I told you before, there's something you have to do first." Eli pointed to an officer standing by a patrol car. "Talk to Ramirez. She's a friend of mine. Give her your statement and tell her you'd like to remain as anonymous as possible. She'll take care of you."

"Okay." Charlie smiled slyly. "Talk to you soon." He spun on his heel before Eli could utter any more denials. He wanted to play it cool as he walked slowly away, putting some extra sway in his hips for good measure, but he couldn't resist the urge to peek back.

When he did, he found Eli watching him with clear desire in his expression. His face snapped back to neutral a second later, but it was too late. Charlie winked at him, and Eli turned quickly away. Charlie thought he spotted a soft smile on Eli's face right before he did, however.

Charlie was halfway to the police officer Eli had indicated when his phone rang. The customized ringtone sent his pulse into overdrive. Of all the places to get a call from him . . . the scene of a crime was a special kind of coincidence.

He was reaching to answer it when one of the reporters behind the barricades spotted him. "Hey, you!"

Charlie could almost see the wheels turning behind the reporter's eyes as he took in Charlie's sooty hair and disheveled clothes.

"Sir," he shouted, "were you in the gym at the time of the fire? What happened? Did it look like foul play?"

The other reporters took notice and shouted questions too, shoving microphones in his direction.

He was still far enough away that they probably couldn't make out his features, thank God. He dropped his eyes to the ground and scuttled behind a tree. Once there, he did something he'd learned to do quite well over the years: disappear. Hopefully, no one would remember he'd ever been there.

His phone stopped ringing. For all of two seconds. Then, the same ringtone blared again. Charlie was going to have a hell of a time explaining where he'd been, and in his line of work, no excuse was good enough. Not even *I ran into a burning building*.

He's gonna blow up my phone until I answer. Might as well get this over with.

Right before he picked up the call, Charlie allowed himself a quiet moment to clutch his phone tightly and bask in the knowledge that Eli's number was inside it.

Maybe he was a hopeless optimist, but he fully believed that in twenty-four hours, he was going to talk to Eli, and they were going to set up a date. If Eli still tried to play off the connection between them . . . Well, Eli had said himself that Charlie was stubborn.

Charlie might have to take matters into his own hands.

Miraculously, in all the time he was away getting flirted with, no one had noticed Eli's absence. Now that the fire was out, their jobs transformed from high-octane action to a lot of standing around and comparing notes with the other first responders.

Relieved as Eli was, his chest tightened when he approached Rogers only to be told there was nothing left to do. They'd made absolutely certain the fire was out, checked the building's structural integrity, and accounted for all the students and faculty. Now it was time for an arson investigator from the police's forensic team to figure out what had caused it. Eli wasn't needed. None of them were.

The aftermath of a call was always a mixed bag for Eli, even when he hadn't fucked up and allowed himself to get distracted. He was usually either exhausted or pumped up, depending on what had happened. In this case, it was the latter, and he had a healthy dose of guilt to go with all his extraneous energy.

That culminated in him nearly vibrating out of his skin as they all piled back into the truck and drove off. By the time they returned to the station, it was . . . still morning. He had almost a full shift ahead of him and nothing to do except find ways to waste time. Unless they got another call.

I refuse to let myself wish that another building would catch on fire, Eli thought as he went to his locker and stowed his equipment. *But if that did happen, I could probably put it out single-handed, I'm so wired.*

A nagging voice in the back of his head told him that if he'd gotten Charlie's number, he could be flirting with him right now. He dismissed it. He'd crossed a major line simply by encouraging Charlie.

Even if they had exchanged contact information, he doubted his moral compass would allow him to act before their twenty-four hours were up.

Although, there was no denying there was a part of him that was praying Charlie would get in touch. It wasn't every day he met cute men on the job, let alone ones who were quick to make a move. And persistent.

Charlie was a bit of a mystery. One second, he was shyly staring at his shoes. The next, he was grabbing Eli's arm and asking him out with swagger. Eli could still feel the imprint of Charlie's fingers in his forearm. Charlie seemed to be an unusual mixture of both quiet and confident. Nondescript and unforgettable. Unassuming and charming. Qualities that shouldn't go together and yet somehow did.

It made it difficult for Eli to get a good initial read on him, but honestly, that only enhanced the mystery. Eli could lie to himself all he wanted, but deep down, he wanted to get to know Charlie more.

Now all he could do was wait and see if he got the chance.

As always, Chief Sappenfield wanted a full report. Rogers gave it with input from the rest of them, although Eli's contribution was notably lacking. It didn't help that he kept ninety percent of his encounter with Charlie to himself.

Lead settled in his gut when the chief frowned at him. She didn't ask for elaboration, however. She dismissed them all and disappeared back into the dispatch office. He'd expected Anette to pounce on him the second the chief left, but shockingly, she went straight to work on her share of the chores. Eli didn't trust that for a microsecond.

Now jittery with both nerves and energy, Eli busied himself for the remainder of his shift washing Dottie III—which, true to form, had somehow gotten covered in mud—and getting in a good workout. The burn in his muscles soothed the guilty ache in his gut and gave him a sense of productivity.

By the time he got home, he was ready for bed, despite the early hour. His cats were almost precisely where he'd left them, though Pistol was now in front of the stove. He had an uncanny and inherently feline ability to lie in front of whatever Eli planned to use next in his kitchen.

"Hey, y'all. Did you miss me?" He locked the door behind himself and deposited his keys onto the kitchen table.

He received a combination of slow blinks, meows, and indifference in response. At least Moxie bothered to rub against both his legs before she sashayed pointedly over to her empty food dish.

"All right, you moochers. Gimme a chance to get out of my work clothes."

Eli settled into his familiar evening routine, which consisted of cooking himself dinner, texting Anette, and cuddling on the couch with Pistol, who camped out in his lap. He remembered wanting to check in with his dad and did so. They had a fifteen-minute conversation about Dad's last doctor's appointment and the ever-rising cost of stamps. When Eli hung up, he somehow felt lonelier than he had before.

After that, he wasted some time on Grindr—though it was usually full of nothing but white country boys asking him if his dick lived up to the stereotype—but even the tolerable ones couldn't hold his interest.

It was an evening like a hundred others he'd had in the past few years. The only difference was, when he got into bed that night—Moxie warming his feet and Chutzpah meowing his head off as he did every evening for around ten minutes—Eli's thoughts turned immediately to Charlie. He pictured Charlie's dark eyes ringed with inky eyelashes, his gorgeous face streaked with soot, and his smile, warm as a breaking dawn.

For the first time in a long time, Eli drifted off to sleep without effort.

Despite how early he'd gone to bed, his alarm seemed to go off as soon as he'd closed his eyes. He fumbled for where he'd placed his phone on the nightstand and swiped blearily at the screen until the noise stopped.

Instantly, Pistol waddled into the room, mewling at the top of his little kitty lungs. It was one of many things Eli loved about his cats: they didn't get loud until *after* his alarm had gone off. Granted, they caused a hell of a ruckus as soon as it did, but it was almost like they knew how important it was for him to be well rested.

"Yeah, yeah," he muttered. "Morning to you too."

Sitting up in bed, he rubbed his eyes and willed himself to find the energy to roll to his feet. Instead, he grabbed his phone and spent a moment fucking around on it, preparing himself for the fact that he was now awake. His groggy brain got lost in the usual social media notifications and junk emails, but then, an icon that looked like a speech bubble caught his eye. His pulse skipped like a scratched CD.

He tapped eagerly on his texts. There were two, one from the chief, and one from an unknown number. His heart sprang up into his throat. Charlie. He went directly for the second text, tapping it with his thumb so hard his knuckle cracked.

Hey, Eli. It's Charlie. I know I said I'd wait twenty-four hours, but hopefully eighteen is good enough. Told you I wouldn't change my mind.

The text ended with a wink emoji. Pure sunshine flooded into Eli. He felt so light, he might float up to the ceiling, Mary Poppins–style.

I knew it. I knew I'd hear from him. I may not believe in jinxes, but fate is starting to look pretty good.

It was a complete lie, but he was too happy to care. A dozen possible responses flashed through his head. While he mentally crafted the perfect reply, he checked the text from Chief Sappenfield.

His happiness died in his chest as he read the message once, twice, three times.

Report to the station ASAP. The police have sent over the results of their preliminary investigation. They believe yesterday's fire was the work of a known serial arsonist. We're on high alert.

CHAPTER 3

When Eli sprinted into the fire station, he found Chief Sappenfield standing before a half-moon of gathered people. Apparently, Eli wasn't the only one the chief had summoned. Both the first and second crews were in attendance. This was the second station-wide meeting Eli had ever seen, and judging by the grim looks on everyone's faces, it wasn't going to be a lively event.

Eli and a few other stragglers joined the crowd. Everyone was silent as they waited for the chief to speak.

She cleared her throat. "In case anyone hasn't read the email I sent out this morning, the lead investigator on this case—Detective Thorpe—has officially declared yesterday's fire an act of arson. The accelerant found at the scene confirms it, and in addition, it matches the MO of a string of fires that occurred three years ago in suburban Louisville. Some of you know them well."

Eli certainly did. Back then, he'd been at the station for a little over a year and had still been considered a new recruit, despite all his volunteer experience. The fires had occurred during a particularly hot, dry summer. Over the course of four weeks, Louisville had been terrorized by four high-profile fires. Then, out of nowhere, they'd simply stopped.

A full-scale investigation had been launched, but nothing had ever come of it. It'd been a priority case, because each fire had been set in a public, populated area. A mall, a movie theater, a park, and a bus station.

Now, they could add an elementary school to the list. Eli's gut churned as Chief Sappenfield cleared her throat again and continued.

"The good news is, it's the rainy season. It should be easier for us to keep any attempts at arson contained. The bad news is, that's all we can do. The police have very few leads, and if they don't catch this guy soon, we have to assume he'll strike again. Detective Thorpe wants our departments to cooperate fully, and of course, we've agreed. For the foreseeable future, it's business as usual, but please double-check all your equipment, and keep the tanks full. Now more than ever, we need to be ready."

Murmurs broke out from the crowd. Eli didn't join them, worry gnawing at his guts. With so little information, it was easy to feel lost. The chief had referred to the arsonist as *he*, but that was just because it was statistically more likely to be a man. In truth, it could be anyone.

Why had the arsonist mysteriously disappeared before? Was he a fire bug, or did he have some sort of insidious purpose? Why attack a *school*, of all the horrible things to do, and where would he strike next?

Eli's head spun with questions. He didn't notice Chief Sappenfield approaching until she was right in front of him.

"Johnson." Her brown eyes, framed in tasteful makeup, were uncharacteristically soft. "You all right?"

"Yes." His voice was raspy. He swallowed. "Why?"

"You look like you're going to be sick."

Eli forced a smile. "I'm fine."

She shook her head. "Don't lie. I know you worked these fires before, and the one from yesterday was no picnic. You don't have to apologize for being upset that this bastard's back."

"The police are sure it's him?" Eli hated to allow himself a shred of hope, but he had to ask. "It couldn't be a mistake?"

"Everything matches perfectly. The same generic household chemicals were used as accelerants, it happened early in the morning exactly like before, the same type of location was chosen, and the police found a shoe print at the scene. Men's size eleven, like the one found at the bus station three years ago. It's not a DNA match, but they're confident the serial arsonist has come out of hiding."

"Why now? After all these years? For that matter, why do this at all?" Eli shook his head. "I know it's silly for me to still be asking these questions after years of working here. Lord knows, I've seen enough people do terrible things for insurance or revenge or whatever. But I don't think it'll ever make sense to me."

"Good." She gave his shoulder a light, brief squeeze: her version of a hug. "I'm no therapist, but I recommend you talk to someone. When I come home after a long day, talking to my husband genuinely helps."

Eli had met Chief Sappenfield's husband at a few station barbecues. He was a funny German guy whose opening line had been to comment on the irony of hosting a barbecue outside a fire station. Eli had almost choked on a rib.

I'd kill to have someone like that in my life. Someone who can make me laugh, who I can lean on when I need strength, and let them lean on me in return.

A realization tapped him on the shoulder: he'd never texted Charlie back. In his rush to get to the station and hear the news, he'd completely forgotten.

"Thanks for the advice, Chief," he said, hand inching toward where his phone rested in his pocket. "I'll consider it."

She nodded and strode off toward the stairs, probably with the intention of seeing if anyone hanging out in the communal area needed a pep talk. He watched her go, and as soon as she'd disappeared, his eyes drifted over the crowd of people leftover.

Anette was standing next to McPherson. She caught his eye and raised a brow in a subtle signal. Thanks to many years of working around loud sirens, they'd gotten very good at nonverbal communication. He heard her voice in his head clear as day. *Everything all right?*

He shook his head.

She jerked hers toward the front doors. *Want to get out of here and talk about it?*

He pulled out his phone and held up a finger. *In a minute.*

She nodded and turned back to McPherson, who had been talking this whole time without noticing he'd lost his audience.

The parking lot was the only place Eli could get any semblance of privacy while both crews occupied the station. He walked outside and was grateful when the sun clapped two warm hands on his shoulders.

Unlike yesterday, today was clear and beautiful, but still cool enough to let him know spring wasn't going anywhere.

Eli leaned against his car and pulled up the text Charlie had sent him. Upon seeing it again, he hesitated. Here Charlie had sent him this cute message, and now Eli was about to fuck up his day by telling him grim news. There was a serial arsonist on the loose, and the trauma Charlie had experienced yesterday was likely to happen to someone else soon.

Should I keep this to myself?

That would go against the advice the chief had given him, but then Charlie wasn't his partner. They hadn't so much as been on a date yet. It wasn't Charlie's job to ease Eli's burdens. Then again, he had to say *something*, or Charlie would think he wasn't interested, and there was precious little else on Eli's mind at the moment. Charlie was sure to see the news on TV anyway, right?

He hesitated for a moment longer before typing a simple message. *I've never been more thrilled to be wrong. How are you?*

There. Short and sweet. Eli would see what Charlie said back, assuming he responded. He was probably busy at work.

Almost the second the message sent, a speech bubble popped up, indicating that Charlie was typing. Damn, that was fast. Eli's heart rate doubled as he waited for a message to appear. He didn't have to wait long.

I'm having a hell of a day. Work is miserable. Are you on duty?

Eli quickly replied. *You know it, and my day's not going much better. Play hooky with me?*

Well damn, that was tempting. Getting out of the office, so to speak, and spending the day with a cute, fun guy? Eli would have loved nothing more, but Chief Sappenfield had said they all needed to be ready for when the arsonist inevitably struck again. If Eli ran off while a serial criminal was on the loose, that would make him both a terrible person and probably unemployed.

I can't. Comes with the territory. You never know when we might get a call.

This time, a speech bubble didn't automatically appear. Eli's pulse fluttered. What if Charlie thought he was the most boring person ever? Or that he was brushing him off? He should have thought more carefully about his response.

Before Eli could panic in earnest, Charlie wrote back.

That responsible streak of yours is so sexy.

Eli actually chuckled out loud. Charlie had to be teasing him. *I find that hard to believe.*

No, it's true. I'm not a reckless person, but I'm not as responsible as I could be. It's a quality I admire in others. And of course, I'm picturing you wrapping me up in your strong arms, all safe and protected. Definitely sexy.

Warmth bloomed in Eli's chest and spread throughout him. Damn, Charlie was smooth as fuck, but there was no doubt in Eli's head that he was being sincere. Was this going a little too easily, though? Or had Eli simply spent too many years keeping one ear cocked for alarm bells? Before he could decide, Charlie sent another message.

I won't ask you to skip work, but you must get a lunch break. Have coffee with me? Around noon?

On days like today, when Eli hadn't brought a lunch from home, he ate in the communal kitchen. Well, unless Thorogood was cooking. The man was a hell of a firefighter, but Lord above, he could fuck up toast. Anette was a good cook, but she was only one person. The rest of the guys were always making shit that was way fattier and red-meatier than Eli preferred. God forbid he brought in a green salad and some salmon. It wasn't *manly* to have unclogged arteries and healthy skin. Getting a break from station food sounded amazing right now.

Eli wrote back. *I'm in. Where do you want to meet?*

Charlie's response was nigh instant. *Are we grabbing a quick drink, or can you sit down and have a meal?*

I can do food or maybe smoothies or something.

He received several cry-laughing emojis along with a message: *I eat like a horse. I don't get people who think kale juice and protein powder is a meal. Meet me at the Corner Store?*

That was a grocery store and deli with a little café inside that Eli knew well. It served homemade jalapeño mac and cheese that he dreamed about when he was watching his carbs. Awesome choice.

See you then. Looking forward to it.

As Eli headed back into the station, he could actually feel the spring in his step. While everyone else was tense and gloomy, he had to stop himself from whistling while he helped wash Dottie III and the second newer engine, Rusty.

Time passed surprisingly quickly, considering how often he checked his phone. When 11:45 rolled around, he told the chief he needed food, assured Anette they'd talk when he got back, and left with his radio clipped to his belt.

The short drive to the Corner Store was sunny and peaceful. Or perhaps everything seemed brighter because he was so eager to get there. Although, when he pulled into the parking lot and spotted Charlie waiting for him outside the store, a sudden wave of nerves swelled up in him.

Charlie looked hot in dark jeans and a nice blue sweater with the sleeves pushed up to his elbows. Now that his face and hair weren't all soot-streaked, it was easier to make out his features. Sharp jaw, absent of stubble. Nice lips. A little on the pale side, but not pasty. He had dark moles on his neck that Eli immediately wanted to kiss.

Play it cool. He's into you, so let him work for it. But be sure to throw him a bone, because damn, *he's fine.*

Eli got out of his car and trotted over. Charlie spotted him right away and met him halfway.

"Hey." Charlie's gorgeous smile was back. His eyes practically sparkled. "Thanks for meeting me."

"Thanks for inviting me. And for getting in touch. I've really never been happier to be wrong."

Charlie reached out and fingered the sleeve of Eli's shirt. "I was expecting to see you in street clothes, but I dig the Louisville FD swag."

Eli looked down at himself. Whoops. He hadn't thought about the fact that he was in his usual blue T-shirt with the department's logo on the chest, and plain pants. He wasn't exactly dressed to impress. Normally, what he wore on dates was a communal decision between him, Anette, and his two nosy aunties. Especially if he was meeting a white boy. "Sorry, I came right from work."

"Don't be. I thought your firefighter outfit was sexy, but this is like a dressed-down version of that." Charlie's fingers trailed to the tattoo that peeked out from under Eli's sleeve. "A crest?"

"Yeah, for the Air Force." Eli considered his words carefully. "Someone important to me was a member. It meant a lot to her."

"And what about this?" Charlie slid the pads of his fingers all the way down to Eli's wrist, giving him goose bumps. "The paw print. Is it for a cat or a dog?"

Eli held back a shiver. "A cat. Three of them actually. I guess you could call me a collector."

Charlie snorted. "I have a tattoo myself."

"Oh?" Eli looked him over. "Where?"

"If the date goes well, you might get to see." He winked and turned toward the shop. "Shall we?"

Eli fell over his own feet in his haste to follow. They stepped inside, and immediately the smell of fresh bread and coffee filled Eli's nose. The Corner Market was considered a new age hippie shop by a good chunk of the locals because it sold organic produce and had nuts instead of candy in the plastic dispensers. Eli, for one, loved it and could eat macadamia nuts by the handful, calories be damned.

Charlie stopped right inside the door and shoved his hands into his pockets. "I'm in the mood for a sandwich from the deli and some coffee. What about you?"

"That sounds good to me. I prefer tea in the afternoon, though."

"Not me. I want a coffee IV drip. Hell, fill the sink, and I'll dunk my head in."

Eli was laughing so hard as they walked toward the deli, he almost didn't notice when Charlie brushed their hands together. He didn't quite lock their fingers, but the intent was there, and it made Eli's skin tingle.

I don't think I've ever had such an easy and instant connection with someone. There has to be an epic downside, right?

No magical answer was forthcoming. They got their food and drinks, found a little table in the café area away from everyone else, and dug in.

For a moment, they were quiet while they chewed. Eli was surprised by how not-awkward it felt. Normally, he'd be scrambling for small talk, but with Charlie, he was content to let the conversation start when it was ready.

After a few bites, Charlie put his sandwich down and fixed Eli in his dark gaze. "So, Eli, tell me about yourself."

"Where would you like me to start?"

"Vocation seems like a good jumping-off point. What made you want to be a firefighter? Childhood dream?"

Eli fought back a flinch. It was a question he got all the time, and he had a number of fake answers that he gave to acquaintances or hookups. They were all rooted in semi-truths, so he wasn't *technically* lying, but it didn't seem right to give one of his bullshit answers to Charlie. Then again, the truth was too sad of a topic for a first date.

He deflected with a genuine curiosity of his. "You've mentioned my job a handful of times now, right down to the 'sexy' uniform. You don't have a thing for firefighters, do you?"

Please say no. That's exactly the sort of red flag I've been waiting for.

Charlie chuckled. "No, I swear I'm not an ambulance chaser or fascinated with fire or anything like that. There's only one firefighter I have a thing for." He smiled. "I asked because I'm interested in you, not what you do."

That was a damn good answer. Eli was quiet as he calculated his next move.

He must've taken too long, because Charlie frowned. "Is something wrong? You don't have to tell me if you'd rather not. I sense there's something you're not saying."

Eli really didn't want to lie, and Charlie was so damn sweet. "It's kind of heavy. I don't want to be a downer."

Charlie reached across the table and brushed his fingers over the back of Eli's hand. "You don't have to tell me, but I promise you won't scare me off. I can handle heavy."

He's impossible to resist.

Eli nodded. "You know how I said someone important to me was in the Air Force?"

"Yeah." Charlie tilted his head to the side. "You said 'she.' Was it a wife or a girlfriend? Hopefully not a current one."

That was almost enough to make Eli smile. "No, it was my mom. She died."

Charlie looked stricken. "Eli, I'm so sorry."

"Don't be. It was a long time ago."

"How long?"

"My brain says eight years, though my heart thinks it happened yesterday." Eli hesitated before turning his hand over to hold Charlie's.

"She had a long battle with breast cancer, and after lots of ups and downs, even she couldn't fight anymore. In the last years of her life, I wanted to drop out of college and take care of her, but she was completely against that. She wanted me to stay in school no matter what. So I did. I listened to her, and it ended up being one of the biggest regrets of my life. I'd give anything to have had more time with her."

Charlie didn't interrupt or ask questions. He just skimmed his fingers over Eli's palm and listened with sympathy—but not pity—in his eyes.

"After she died, I ended up dropping out anyway. I'd been studying engineering before that, but losing her made me reevaluate my life. Luckily, I come from a strong community, and there were a lot of people—relatives and family friends—who supported me.

"Mom was always saying that the best thing you can do is leave the Earth better than it was before. That was why she joined the Air Force. I wanted to follow in her footsteps in my own way, so I decided to become a firefighter. That's why I'm always insisting I'm not a hero. I'm just trying to do a little bit of good, whenever I can. And now, here I am." He laughed, but it sounded flat. "I swear I don't normally talk about this on first dates. Or at all. Sorry for spilling my soul."

"Don't be. It's a good soul." Charlie squeezed his hand. "I'm glad you told me. Your mom sounds like she was an incredible person."

"She was. Inside and out." Eli grabbed his phone and scrolled to a photo of a photo: the one on his fridge. He held it out for Charlie to see.

Charlie's lips twitched up. "Not to sound the absolute gayest, but oh my god, I *love* her hair."

Eli, who'd taken a sip of his tea, almost spat it out. "You have the best sense of humor."

"Thanks. I make jokes to hide how secretly awkward I am." Charlie took another bite of his sandwich and washed it down with coffee. "I like your hair too, by the way."

Eli couldn't stop himself from snorting.

Charlie raised a brow. "What?"

"Nothing."

"Eli. Tell me."

Eli shrugged. "It's really nothing. I'll just never understand white folks' fascination with black hair."

Charlie squawked. "I only said I like yours. That's hardly 'fascination.'"

"Uh-huh." Eli fought back a grin. "Be honest. Were you thinking about touching it?"

"I . . . Fuck." Charlie sat back in his chair. "You win. It looks so soft, though. Do I get points for resisting the urge?"

"Absolutely. I hate when random people touch my head."

"All right. I promise to never do that." He paused for coffee and then cleared his throat. "I suppose I should tell you about myself, since you opened up to me."

"I'd like that. Let's start simple. What do you do for a living?"

Charlie looked away, fidgeting in his seat. "Oh, my job is super boring. Lots of paperwork and sitting at a desk. It's nothing compared to yours."

Eli pursed his lips at Charlie's clear evasiveness. "So, is it like an office job, or what?"

"You could say that." Charlie took another bite, spent a long moment chewing, and then flashed a too-bright smile. "I'm curious: how does one go about becoming a firefighter? Do you go to a special fire school, or what?"

That was a blatant misdirection, but Eli let it go. If Charlie didn't want to talk about his job, it must be with good reason. Though, considering Eli had been waiting for a red flag to pop up, it didn't bode well.

"It's actually a lot easier than you might think. Well, to volunteer, at least. To get a paid position, you have to have a high school diploma, pass all the prehire tests, and then you get put on a list of eligible potential new hires by local fire departments. After that, you cross your fingers and wait. At least, that's how it works in Kentucky."

"Are you from here?"

"Nah, I've lived here since high school. We moved all over when my mom was in the Air Force, but then she got sick and wanted to be closer to family. I was opposed to coming here, actually. When I found out we were moving somewhere conservative and almost all white, I thought we were going to be miserable. But now it's home, and with the exception of the occasional racist asshole, I love Louisville."

Charlie nodded. "Makes sense. I've lived here my whole life, and oh boy, do I know how people can be. It's beautiful, but this is the Bible Belt. Ignorant rednecks literally come with the territory. I dunno if this puts you at ease or anything, but you're not the first black guy I've dated. If we walk down the street holding hands and get some stares, it's not going to be news to me."

Eli nodded. "We'd get stared at for a lot more than you being white. There's the gay thing too. A double whammy."

"Well, if they don't like it, they can look away." Charlie shrugged. "I'm not scared." He took Eli's hand again.

Eli squeezed it before leaning back. "Me neither. So, tell me something else about you. Break a dating rule so I feel better about breaking one." He used the opportunity to take a big bite of his food. He'd been so busy talking, he hadn't had a chance to eat.

"Um, let me think." Charlie tapped his chin. "Talking about exes seems like a similar first-date no-no. In truth, it's been a long time since I've had a serious boyfriend. Like, a good few years."

Eli swallowed quickly. "I find that hard to believe. You're hot and funny, and you're not afraid to make the first move."

"Oh, you were an exception, trust me. I'm not usually inspired enough to ask a guy out that directly. But yeah, my last boyfriend was years ago. I was in my final year of college, and I'd been embroiled in this dramatic relationship with a guy named Louis. We fought all the time, but I thought it was passion, and he made me laugh."

"Was he as funny as you?"

"Oh, funnier. No contest." Charlie put on a super serious face. "One time, he told this joke over dinner that made me laugh so hard, wine came out of my nose. Which was weird, because I wasn't even drinking wine."

Eli fucking lost it. He had to cover his mouth to keep from causing a ruckus. "Oh my God, there's no way he was funnier than you."

Shrugging, Charlie grinned. "Maybe not, but he was very good at making me laugh when I was trying to be furious with him. I think I stayed much longer than I should have because of that. It didn't end well."

"What happened?"

"When graduation rolled around, he wanted to move in together, and I wanted to take a break. We ended up deciding to mutually call it off but remain friends. It worked for a while, but then we got into an argument over something stupid, and he had this public meltdown on my Facebook. Remember back when people still fought through social media? It wasn't pretty."

"So, you unfriended him?"

"Oh no, I tried to talk things out like the naïve little after-school special I am. He blocked me, and I haven't heard from him since."

"Yikes. He lives in Louisville?"

"No, thank God. Last I heard, he moved." Charlie waved. "Good riddance, as far as I'm concerned. Anyway, after that, I threw myself into work, and I haven't dated anyone seriously since. Though, I'm hoping that changes soon."

What a flirt. I love it.

A second later, the first part of what he'd said caught up with Eli. "Wait, you threw yourself into work? Your office job that you said isn't worth talking about? Wouldn't that be super boring?"

Charlie suddenly stood up. "Excuse me for a second. That coffee went straight through me. I'll be right back." He scurried toward the back of the store, where bathrooms signs were mounted on the walls.

Eli stared after him, thoughts churning. When Charlie had been evasive before, Eli had thought he was being coy, or maybe avoiding a painful subject. But they'd crossed that threshold now. His continued refusal to talk about his job was getting downright weird.

I don't want to push him, though. Not on a first date. Should I trust that he has a good reason? Am I being paranoid? I've always gone with my gut, but in this case, I'm not sure what to do.

He scarfed down the rest of his lunch while he had the chance. At least if things got awkward, and he needed to make a quick getaway, he wouldn't go hungry. Depending on how the day went, he might end up eating whatever the kitchen had whipped up as well. Workouts always left him ravenous.

Before long, Charlie reappeared, a sweet smile on his face. "Back. How was your sandwich?"

It was hard to be paranoid when looking at such a cute man. "Really good. I'd never had one from here before. I usually go straight for the jalapeño mac and never look back."

"Oh my *God*." Charlie clasped his hands together like an old-timey movie star. "I *live* for their mac. I had to make it a special-occasions-only food, or I was going to get scurvy."

Eli laughed. "Relatable."

"Seriously though, my mom and I have lunch together once a week, and she always wants to come here. It's dangerous, because I can drop fifty bucks on fancy cheese alone if I'm not careful."

"You have lunch with your mom every week? That's ridiculously adorable."

"We're a pretty close-knit clan. I have an older sister who lives nearby, and she brings her husband and the kids over to Mom's house for dinner at least once a month. We get together for holidays and birthdays too. It's a lot of fun." Charlie smiled crookedly, and one of his cheeks dimpled.

"You have the most gorgeous smile." Eli leaned forward. "Do you—"

A scream ripped through the relative quiet of the store. Eli's head jerked instinctively toward it. In the back, he spotted the last thing he'd expected to see pouring out from beneath one of the doors.

Smoke.

Seconds later, the fire alarm pierced the air and his eardrums. Eli jumped to his feet at the same time Charlie did. Panic broke out, but in the center of the chaos, the two of them stared at each other, a calm eye in a rising storm. The dread on Charlie's face told Eli they'd come to the same conclusion.

Another fire.

CHAPTER 4

The alarms sent Eli straight into damage-control mode. He surveyed the store quickly, assessing the situation. There were two dozen people inside, counting employees, and the smoke was coming from the back right corner. If everyone exited calmly out the front, they'd all be fine. The problem was, in Eli's experience, crowds of people were exactly like scared horses. They tended to spook.

As if on cue, someone screamed again. Panicked voices rose over the smoke alarm, and people started surging toward the front, preparing to stampede.

Eli held up his arms and shouted, "Everyone, remain calm. I'm Firefighter Johnson with the Louisville FD. Everything's going to be fine. Exit calmly through the front doors, don't run, and cover your mouths if you can."

The smoke was intensifying by the second, but luckily, Eli's presence seemed to calm everyone. He had to admit, it was apropos. It was like having a cop pop up while you were being robbed, or a handy off-duty paramedic at the scene of a car accident.

Some of the tension in the room was dispelled, and people filed relatively uniformly toward the front doors. A passing employee directed Eli to where the fire extinguishers were located and told him the sprinklers were on a timer. They would activate if the alarm wasn't turned off within a few minutes. Eli had no idea how to reset the system, and honestly, he'd rather keep it armed, just in case.

"You'd better get out of here too," Eli shouted to Charlie over the din, pointing to the thinning crowd jostling out the doors. "I'll see what's up."

Charlie hesitated, a frown on his face. "Can I help? It could be dangerous."

Eli's heart was already beating like a drum, but at that, he recognized the surge of adrenaline that was also coursing through him. It lit his nerve endings up like a chandelier. Standing this close to Charlie, danger thick in the air, made him dizzy in ways that had nothing to do with the smoke. Part of him wanted to grab Charlie by his handsome, brave face and kiss him, but now wasn't the time.

He touched Charlie's shoulder, the barest of consolation prizes. "Definitely a hero. But seriously, I shouldn't even check it out without gear or backup. My chief's gonna have my ass. I'll call for help—" Eli unclipped the radio on his belt and held it up "—and pray that she's so impressed with my quick action, she forgets to fire me. The station probably already got the alarm. When I'm done, I'll meet you outside."

"Okay." Charlie's expression was a portrait of reluctance as he turned away. "But if you're not out in five minutes, I'm coming after you."

I could eat him up with a spoon.

Eli watched to make sure Charlie left, before jogging toward the customer service desk. Just as the employee had said, a fire extinguisher was mounted to the nearby wall. He grabbed it and sprinted to the back of the store. A glance told him which door the smoke was coming from, and for a moment, his heart stopped.

The men's bathroom.

Charlie had left that bathroom mere minutes before the smoke had appeared. Eli's brain worked sluggishly to process that information. What did this mean?

Could he ... Could Charlie have ...

Eli shoved his thoughts aside. Not now. He had work to do.

Covering his nose and mouth with his shirt, he kicked the door open. Smoke poured out in billowing gray plumes. He crouched low and crept forward, squinting to see through the murk. Inside the bathroom, the smoke was pouring out of one of those big plastic garbage cans as if it were a witch's cauldron. From its mouth, it spat the occasional tongue of flame up toward the blackening ceiling.

Luckily, it was surrounded by tile walls and floors, so the fire hadn't spread. The plastic can had melted like a candle from the heat, however, and would soon collapse. When that happened, it would either fizzle out or lick up the wooden stalls to the ceiling. Eli wasn't willing to find out.

He pulled the pin on the fire extinguisher, aimed the black hose toward the flames at a low angle, and squeezed the handle. What looked like white fog erupted from the nozzle. Eli swept it side to side, coating the trash can inside and then out. He did his best not to breathe in either the extinguishing agent or the smoke, though it was a nigh futile effort.

When he was confident the fire was out, he peered into the lopsided can. Or rather, what remained of it. There was a blackened mess at the bottom mixed with ash and crumbled brown bits. Paper towels, maybe? Had someone purposefully lit the trash can on fire, or was this an accident?

Eli was reluctant to jump to conclusions, considering how many accidental fires he'd seen people set. Most folks would be surprised to learn how easy it was to start a fire, considering how difficult it looked in camping movies. Sometimes all it took was one inconsiderate employee deciding to sneak a cigarette in the bathroom. If someone had thrown a butt into a trash can full of paper towels, it could smolder for hours before finally blazing up.

But what if this wasn't an accident? This could be the work of the serial arsonist. Eli's pulse raced as possibilities popped into his head. *He always picks public places, and a well-known lunch spot is a perfect fit. If so, it's his bad luck that a firefighter happened to be here while he was making his move.*

Something about that bothered Eli. What were the chances? And there was a much bigger coincidence going on: Charlie had been at the scene of both fires.

Louisville wasn't a small city. With a population topping half a million, the probability of any one random citizen being present at both fires was astronomical. Plus, Charlie had been in the bathroom minutes before the smoke had appeared. Could he have set the fire?

Eli huffed a breath. That was ridiculous. Charlie had been right in front of Eli when the smoke had appeared. There hadn't been enough time for him to set a fire, come back, sit down, and talk for several minutes before the smoke appeared.

Unless he'd used a slow accelerant, or a cigarette, or . . .

"There's no way." Eli bodily cleared his thoughts with a shake. He spoke out loud as if giving a pep talk. "No fucking way. I can't—I can't even think it. It's a coincidence. It has to be. I'm *not* dating the serial arsonist."

His voice sounded hollow as it bounced off the bland tile walls. Recalling Charlie's threat to come looking for him if he was gone for too long, Eli set the fire extinguisher down and exited the bathroom. Two seconds after he got back into the main store, the sprinklers went off. Water gushed down on him from the ceiling. Eli stood still for a moment, cursing vehemently in his head, before he held his arms out in resignation.

Yep, this might as well happen.

Not even attempting to shield himself, he trudged toward the front of the store. He was soaked through by the time he reached the glass doors.

Outside, he was greeted by a much larger crowd than he'd anticipated; some busybodies had probably spotted the smoke while driving past and had stopped to investigate. Charlie was right up front, his face twisted with so much concern, guilt stabbed Eli in the sternum.

It can't be him.

Charlie rushed forward. "Is everything all right?"

"Yeah, the fire is out. It was a small one. Nothing I couldn't handle."

The crowd applauded, and Eli's face heated.

He pulled his wet shirt from his chest and released it. It sucked back onto his skin with a squelching sound. "Though the sprinkler system still thinks danger is imminent."

Charlie gave him a quick once-over—as if checking for injuries— only to stop and do it again, slower this time. Eli must look like a drowned rat. He started to apologize, but then Charlie hesitantly raised a hand. Eyes still glued to Eli's chest, he took a single finger and dragged it down Eli's torso. The touch was featherlight, and yet through his shirt, Eli felt the heat behind it, literally and figuratively.

He glanced down at himself and realized what Charlie had been staring at. His shirt was plastered to him like a second skin. It might as well have been blue paint. Every muscle in his abdomen—the ones he worked on whenever he had downtime at the fire station, which was often—was outlined in sharp relief.

Eli wasn't vain about his body. He kept fit so in a crisis, he'd be strong enough, fast enough, to maybe make a difference. But he had to admit, he looked good. And having Charlie appreciate it felt *damn* good.

Charlie took a step closer and looked up at him, bottom lip caught between his teeth. Eli met his gaze, and when he did, a shiver zinged down his spine. Charlie's eyes were glazed and dark with arousal, smoldering like the fire Eli had just put out. Only this fire, he very much wanted to keep alive.

Kiss him, he thought as he edged closer on autopilot. *Forget the crowd. Sweep him up into your arms and kiss him like you've wanted to since the moment you got here.*

Charlie seemed to be thinking the same thing, because his eyes trailed down to Eli's mouth and lingered there. Eli swore he could hear his quickened breathing, though that was impossible over the smoke alarm and raised voices.

He was seconds away from sinking a hand into Charlie's thick hair and pulling their mouths together when another voice in the back of his head chimed in.

How can you kiss him and doubt him at the same time? Moments ago, you wondered if he might be the arsonist. Can you be with him without knowing for sure?

Shit.

Eli fell back a step, the spell broken. He scrambled to make his expression neutral, but he had no idea if he'd succeeded.

Charlie blinked at him, arousal quickly shifting to confusion. "Eli, what—"

Eli's radio sprang to life on his belt, cutting off whatever Charlie was going to say. He kept it tuned to the dispatch frequency, so anytime they needed him to show up to a location, he could be there.

"Johnson." It was the chief's voice. "We got a call. There's a fire at—"

He grabbed the radio and hit a button. "Harold Street, the Corner Market. Over."

"Yes. Don't interrupt me. We need you there ASAP. There's no report on how big the fire is, since the call came from their automated sprinkler system, but I want all of the first crew there. Over."

"I'm already here, Chief. The fire's been put out, but someone needs to disable the alarm and sprinklers. Over."

There was a loaded pause. "How could you . . . You know what? Never mind. The rest of your squad will be arriving any minute. I'll tell the second crew to stand down. Did you see anything suspicious? Were there any signs that this was the work of the arsonist? Over."

Eli's eyes flicked over to Charlie. For a moment, he paused, his stomach icing over. Then, he forced his thick tongue to work. "No, Chief. Not that I could see. Over."

"Keep looking. The cavalry's on the way. Over and out."

Clipping his radio back onto his belt, Eli studiously avoided making eye contact with Charlie. "Sounds like a truck is on its way." Words weighed down his tongue. He wasn't sure what to say. He couldn't come out and *ask* if Charlie had started the fire, right? He wanted to, but that wasn't rational, and Charlie would probably be insulted, with good reason.

For the millionth time, he told himself it couldn't be Charlie. Why would someone start a fire while they were on a date? Then again, every blaze caused by the arsonist had been put out relatively quickly, much like this one. The media had always assumed they never got serious because they were all set in public places with lightning-fast response times. But what if the fires weren't *meant* to be destructive?

What if the arsonist didn't care about the actual damage? What if he cared about the attention? What if . . . he was a guy with a hero complex?

In Eli's head, he pictured Charlie, covered in soot, carrying a crying child out of a burning building. A true Good Samaritan. Then he pictured Charlie hanging back while everyone else in the store evacuated, telling Eli he wanted to stay and help.

I don't really believe this, do I? I can't. It's irrational. Charlie was with me when this fire started. It's got to be a coincidence.

"I know what you're thinking."

Eli's eyes snapped over to Charlie's face. "What?"

Charlie's expression was smooth as still water. "You think I'm the arsonist."

Eli almost fell back a step. He opened and closed his mouth several times before managing to echo, "*What?*"

"Come on, Eli. I'm no genius, but you don't have to be to make that connection. I've been at the scene of two fires now. That's suspicious as hell."

For a stunned moment, Eli stared at him in silence. Then he huffed a breath. "All right, I can appreciate your bluntness. You walked out of the men's room minutes before it burst into flames. I'm sorry, but that doesn't look good."

To Eli's surprise, instead of getting angry, Charlie nodded. "I get it. I would have thought the same thing. Maybe my word doesn't mean anything to you, but for the record: I'm not the arsonist. It's a coincidence. An admittedly bizarre one, but a coincidence nonetheless."

Hearing Charlie refute it actually made Eli feel better. "Okay. For the record on my end, the second the thought popped into my head, I told myself it couldn't be you."

"It's okay." Charlie put his hand on Eli's forearm and squeezed. "I'm not thrilled by the idea, but I get it. You're a firefighter. It'd be wrong for you to let whatever you feel for me cloud your judgment."

Eli swallowed thickly and stepped closer. "Right now, I'm thinking you're just about perfect."

Before Charlie could say anything else, his pager went off. He glanced at it briefly and sighed. "I'm sorry, Eli, but I have to go."

"Damn. Was that your work?"

"Yeah, that's it. My lunch break is up. I need to get back to the, uh, office." Charlie finally looked up, eyes soft. "I wish our date hadn't gotten interrupted, but I'm glad I got to see you. It was such good luck that you were here and no one got hurt."

Seriously, Eli scolded himself, *how could you have thought for a second this guy is a criminal? Look at that face. Charlie is sweet, charming, funny, and . . . maybe a little* too *good? Jesus, he's the most promising romantic prospect I've had in years, and I practically accused him of arson. Might be time to get another cat.*

Eli shook his head. "Won't your boss understand when you say the building where you had lunch literally caught on fire? Besides, the police and EMS and all that will be here soon. They're going to want another statement. You know the drill. There will be curious civilians and a whole media circus, like last time."

At that, familiar unease crept across Charlie's features. "I was hoping to duck out before all of the fuss. My boss won't accept anything short of death as an excuse to be late. Besides, I didn't see anything."

The reassurance Eli had felt moments before all but evaporated.

"But the fire started in the men's room." Eli swallowed around a knot forming in his throat. "You must've seen *something*."

Charlie shook his head. "I'm afraid not. I wish I had." Before Eli could react, Charlie swooped in and planted a warm kiss on his cheek. "I had a great time. By far the best date I've ever been on where something caught on fire. I hope we can do this again soon?"

Eli's blood curdled. Charlie looked so handsome as he studied Eli with big, hopeful eyes.

Words tumbled out of Eli's mouth. "Of course. Looking forward to it."

"Wonderful. Talk to you soon." Charlie hurried away, disappearing behind a line of cars.

As soon as Charlie was gone, Eli realized he should have insisted he stay. The police would need to know that Charlie had been present at both crime scenes. Despite his refutation, the fact that he always wanted to skip out before anyone really saw him was shady as fuck.

Okay, so do I believe him or not? This back and forth is making me dizzy.

As Eli searched his feelings, he realized he did believe Charlie deep down. Maybe Eli was a naïve, infatuated fool, but Charlie had confronted the accusation head on, and when he'd said he wasn't the arsonist, his voice had been steady. If he was a liar, he was a damn good one.

Maybe there's something else going on with him. Some other reason why he doesn't want to be caught at the scene of a crime. Whatever it is, it can't be good.

Especially since there was no denying the connection between Charlie and him. Eli could still feel where Charlie had dragged a finger down his chest. If that simple touch could turn Eli on, he could only imagine what it'd be like to kiss Charlie. Hold him. Be naked with him. Spread him out on a bed, and—

A siren blared as a fire truck appeared at the end of the street. It raced down to the market, police and EMS hot on its tail. Naturally, after the cavalry came, the ambulance chasers appeared. The Channel 8 news van sped into view like a herald of doom. The reporter—a young white man who looked like he'd never outgrown his hipster phase—hopped out of the car before it'd come to a complete stop and sprinted for the crowd.

Please don't see me, Eli thought a split second before the reporter's eyes landed on him. Ugh. It was Peter Lester too. A notorious ambulance chaser. One look at the fire department logo on Eli's shirt, and Lester changed course, barreling toward him. Eli sighed but stood his ground. He'd learned how to handle the media long ago.

"Sir"—Lester shoved a microphone in Eli's face—"is everyone all right? Was this the work of the Louisville arsonist?"

Eli fixed him with a pointed look. "How are you going to interview me when your cameraman is still in the van?" He nodded to the news van that had finally screeched up to the curb. Another young man was struggling to haul equipment out of the back, including a big movie-style camera.

Lester glanced back and cursed, the microphone dangling limply from his hand. "Goddamn it, Jerry. You want Channel 10 to scoop us?"

Seconds later, several police officers appeared and ushered him away, including a woman who caught him by the scruff of his neck like a kitten and practically tossed him behind one of the barricades that had been hastily put into place. Other reporters popped up next to him seconds later, and the clamoring began.

Eli rolled his eyes. *I get why the press is important, but sometimes, I fucking hate the press.*

Anette jumped out of the truck and jogged up to him. "Eli! What happened? Chief told us you were already here. Are you okay?"

"I breathed in some serious fumes, but otherwise ..." Eli hesitated. He'd lied about Charlie once already. Was he going to keep doing it? He could end up digging a hell of a hole for himself if he was wrong about Charlie and later it was discovered Eli had dated an arsonist.

That was the sort of scandal that could lead to him losing his job, or worse, people getting hurt. The photo of his mother in her Air Force uniform, smiling so proudly, flashed into his mind.

"Anette, I need to tell you something."

"What are you—"

"Not here." He let out a tight breath. "You're not going to like it."

As Charlie fought to open his front door—the goddamn lock stuck more and more every day—he spoke to the young black man waiting patiently next to him, "Technically speaking, lying by omission isn't the same thing as flat-out lying."

"Honey, it ain't telling the truth neither," replied Amos, Charlie's best friend and occasional biggest critic. He was lounging against the corridor wall with one sneakered foot flat against it. The lock groaned, and he nodded at the door. "You need some help with that?"

"Nah, I got it. I've been weight training." Charlie braced his shoulder against the wood and jiggled the key in the lock. Afternoon light from a nearby window stung his eyes. He hadn't, in fact, gone back to work like he'd told Eli. Instead, he'd called an emergency meeting with the one person he could trust to tell it to him straight. "I get what you're saying, but it's too early for the truth. I'm trying to not scare the poor guy off."

The door finally opened with a worrisome creak, and Charlie tumbled inside, hopping on one foot to keep from landing on his face.

Amos snickered and came in behind him, shutting the door with ease. "The longer you wait, the worse it's gonna get. Besides, if this boy can't handle it, you're better off without him."

"Easy for you to say. You haven't met Eli." Charlie whistled. "He's charming. He's principled. And he's a California ten, coated in Southern sweetness."

"You said he's a brother, right? Maybe I do know him."

"Isn't it racist to assume all black people know each other?"

Amos winked. "Not if you're black, and not in Louisville, where the white population outnumbers the black four to one. It's not gonna matter for long, though. If this boy's as principled as you said, how do you think he's gonna react to your lie? Ah shit, sorry, I mean your *'omission.'*"

Charlie set his keys down on the little table in his entryway with a sigh. His empty apartment greeted him with too-still silence. He lived alone and wasn't a pet person, though he suspected he was going to warm to cats in the near future.

He flipped on some lights for them and surveyed the space. It was more on the cramped side than cozy, with stark white walls, simple furniture, and bland art that'd come with the place. It wasn't how he'd choose to decorate, but he wasn't planning on being here for long.

"I don't know," he answered honestly. "It's not like I *want* to lie. I hate lying. Especially to sweet, sexy firefighters who look serious one second but then laugh at the slightest provocation. I just wanted to go on a normal date with a normal guy, but shit got all complicated."

"'Cause you made it complicated, 'cause you didn't tell the truth from the start."

"Yeah, yeah. You want a beer?"

"You know me, man. Ain't gotta ask me twice."

Off to the left, a table in the kitchen was cluttered with piles of paperwork, folders, coffee mugs, and more. Charlie headed for the kitchen, where Amos bypassed all that and walked straight through to the living room. It featured the typical accoutrements: a red couch, an old TV, and an entertainment center. He took a seat and for once didn't reach immediately for the stereo remote. He must not be done lecturing Charlie yet.

Charlie grabbed two beers, handed one to Amos, and then flopped onto the sofa with a groan. At twenty-six, he was way too young to be this sore at the end of the day, but he'd spent the past eight hours on his feet. He got a pass this once. "You're right. And I know you're right. Although, you know I asked you over for *support*, right?"

Amos scoffed. "You wanted my opinion because you know I'm a good friend, and I'll kick your bony white ass if you need it. Be real, man: even if your boy is magically fine with your 'omission,' how do you think he's going to react to your lil secret? Y'all are at odds on a very basic level here."

"Which is why I don't want to tell him. Not yet, anyway." Charlie's head fell against the back of the sofa. He stared up at the plain white ceiling, thoughts skittering like mice. "If I show him the real me first, I'm sure later, he'll be able to see past how I pay my bills."

"If you say so." The skepticism in Amos's voice was unmistakable. "I hope you know what you're doing."

"Me too, buddy. Me too."

CHAPTER 5

Upon returning to the fire station, Eli's first order of business was to find some privacy and tell Anette everything, but when he walked in, that plan flew out of his head.

Chief Sappenfield was standing in the dispatch office—as usual—but this time, she wasn't alone. A middle-aged white woman was with her, and from the look on her red face, they weren't having a friendly chat.

Eli couldn't pinpoint precisely what it was, but she looked sort of . . . familiar. Not in a way that reassured him, though. Between the stiff set of the chief's shoulders and the fact that he could hear their muffled voices from across the garage, his hackles rose.

He approached the office slowly with the intent of stopping just out of hearing range: not close enough to be accused of eavesdropping, but close enough that he could restrain the mystery woman if need be.

As it turned out, there was no need. A moment later, the woman threw her arms up into the air and shouted, clear as a bell, "Y'all just stay away from me and mine!" Then she about-faced and stormed out of the office.

There was no time for Eli to duck out of sight. As she passed him on her way to the door, she narrowed her eyes and hissed, "Y'all watch yourselves. Or else." Her warpath to the exit was enough to make Rogers dive out of the way.

When she was gone, Anette caught his gaze and raised both eyebrows up to her hairline.

Eli shrugged in response and glanced back at the office. The chief was leaning against a desk with her head back and her eyes closed, as if she were beseeching the Lord for strength. Risking a potential scolding, Eli approached.

"Knock, knock." He poked his head cautiously in the doorway. "Can I ask what that was all about?"

Chief Sappenfield rubbed her temples before cracking one eye open. "*That*—" she paused for emphasis "—was Mrs. Mary Ann Phelan."

"*Phelan*?" Eli's mouth fell open. "As in—"

"As in Billy Ray Phelan's momma, yeah. The man who was brought in for questioning under suspicion of being the serial arsonist three years ago." Chief Sappenfield sighed. "I'm sure you heard the choice words she had for me. For the whole department, actually. She still blames us for what happened to her son."

"That wasn't our fault, though." Eli stepped into the room and lowered his voice. "We had good reason to suspect him. He worked at both the mall and the movie theater where the first fires happened. The police thought he was our guy too. At first, anyway."

Chief Sappenfield held up a hand. "I'm well aware, but considering what happened when the media got hold of the fact that Billy Ray was a suspect, can you blame her for being pissed?"

"I guess not." Eli frowned. "What good is coming down here going to do, though?"

"She wanted to make sure we're not going to come after any more of her family." She shrugged. "Seems kind of pointless, I agree. With these fires starting up again long after her son was run out of town, that pretty much proves Billy Ray's innocence. You'd think she'd be thrilled at the news. But no, that didn't stop her from calling me a dirty Mexican, despite my repeated assurances that my parents are from Puerto Rico."

"Jesus. Maybe we should think about filing a police report, in case she tries anything."

"I wouldn't worry about it." She patted Eli's shoulder. "People do strange things when they're angry or afraid. I'm sure we've seen the last of her."

"You have to call him."

Eli fell dramatically back against the pillows he'd piled behind him on the bed, even though Anette couldn't see him. "I can't. What would I say?"

Next to him on the bed, he'd placed his phone on the rumpled green duvet. A stereo version of Anette's voice tsked at him. "I don't know. The truth, maybe?"

A week had passed since Eli's date with Charlie. The fire at the Corner Market had not been ruled an accident and was believed to be the work of the serial arsonist. Of course.

The news had broken yesterday, and Eli had felt sick ever since. This was the first day he hadn't had to come into the station all week, and he still couldn't enjoy it.

He looked around his room. It was neat, as always, and filled with sunshine. Not the gray, predawn sunshine he was used to, but proper, midmorning light. The kind he saw on the rare occasions when he got a day off.

But as warm sunlight tickled framed photos, the buttery yellow walls, his furniture, and a basket of laundry that needed washing, he couldn't relax. All he seemed to do these days was obsess.

Memories of Charlie and the fires played over and over again in his head, like whatever the modern equivalent of a broken record was. An iTunes library with one song, stuck on repeat, for all eternity.

Anette, on the other hand, seemed unconcerned. It was odd, considering Eli had told her *everything*. His "chance" meeting with Charlie. The chemistry between them. How Charlie had been at both fires. His evasiveness. Everything. And somehow, she'd come out of it as one of Charlie's biggest cheerleaders.

"I can't *date* someone who might be a criminal," Eli argued in the general direction of his phone. "I'm a public servant. I have to set an example."

"I thought you said he told you point-blank he's not the arsonist."

"He did, but that doesn't mean he's not up to something shady. There has to be a reason he's so skittish around cops."

"Why not ask him? He was upfront with you before."

Eli sighed. "Because I already accused him of one crime. If I accuse him of another, I doubt he'll be as cool as he was before. But I can't just keep dating him either. I'm not feeling it."

"Well, that's a lie. Eli, trust me. There's a perfectly logical explanation for all of this, and if you come to him from a place of honesty and communication, I'm sure he'll understand."

"You've been watching talk shows again. I can tell. You still got that thing for Maury?"

". . . Montel."

"Lord." He let his head fall against his headboard with a soft *thunk*. Moxie, who'd been sleeping next to him, opened one eye and gave him the feline approximation of a glare. He mouthed *I'm sorry* at her squashy face.

"Okay, let's think this through, then." There was a rustling sound. Eli imagined Anette getting comfortable on a sofa, folding her fawn-like legs under her petite body. "Say Charlie *is* up to something shady, but it's not arson. What's the worst-case scenario?"

Eli considered it. "He's a murderer or a rapist, I guess."

"Do you actually think for a second that's the case? Because last I checked, murderers don't run into burning buildings to save children."

"No, but a pedophile might," Eli said just to be contrary. "You're right, though. I don't *really* think he's a violent criminal."

"What do you think, then?"

"Well . . ." He chewed on his lower lip. "When I first met him, I noticed he had a pager, and I made a joke about how only doctors and drug dealers have those these days. He sort of brushed off the comment, and it got me thinking. Maybe he deals or something."

Anette made a humming sound. "That would make more sense than him being the arsonist."

"How can you be so sure he's not, though? You don't know the guy, and the evidence against him is pretty damning."

"It's circumstantial at best. And you forget: I met him briefly at the scene of the first fire. I saw the way he looked at you. No way a criminal mastermind who just attacked a school could have stars that bright in his eyes."

Eli couldn't help but smile at the thought of that first meeting. He remembered the heart-pounding excitement he'd felt, not because of the chaos, but because of the handsome, sooty man who'd smiled at him and called him a hero. How had things gone so awry since then?

"You're missing the point, Anette." He exhaled through his teeth. "Even if he's not a criminal mastermind, I still can't associate with him."

"Sure you can. He's a lil white boy who lives in Kentucky. I doubt he runs a heroin cartel. He probably sells weed to his country club friends on the side or something. Most states have legalized that."

"Not Kentucky, and tell that to all the black men still rotting in jail for getting pulled over with a dime bag in their pocket."

Anette whistled. "All right, all right. No need to spill tea on me. I don't think you actually have a problem with the possibility. You're only fixating on it because that's what you do."

Pistol jumped onto the bed and headbutted Eli's hip. Eli reached out and absently patted the cat's fuzzy head. "What do you mean?"

"Thanks to my sociology degree, I'm totally qualified to make this observation." She was using the pseudo-academic voice she affected whenever she talked about college. "You, Eli, are a self-saboteur."

"I am not." He paused. "But out of curiosity, what makes you say that?"

Anette laughed. "I don't know how you got it into your head that you don't deserve nice things, but whenever someone tries to give you a medal, or call you a hero, you insist you're doing what anyone would do. But that's the thing, Eli. Not everyone chooses this life. Not everyone puts themselves in danger every day for others. Sure, you get paid for it, but honestly, if the station hadn't hired you, wouldn't you have volunteered anyway?"

Eli shrugged, and it earned him another glare from Moxie. "I suppose. I don't see what that has to do with Charlie, though."

"You're doing the same thing again. A handsome, charming guy is into you, so naturally you're convinced there must be something wrong with him. It's not about Charlie. It's about you. Charlie wants you, and you can't accept that."

"If that's true, then that's depressing. I really don't think my self-confidence is that low. I like me. I want me to be happy. Why would I sabotage myself?"

"Beats me, but if I had to guess, I'd say it's because you had a role model that you've never felt like you could live up to. Say—oh, I don't know—a heroic parent. Perhaps one who died during your formative years and instilled in you the idea that doing good is expected, not celebrated? And you're constantly trying to fill shoes that no one expects you to fill? This is pure conjecture, of course."

"Uh-huh." Eli blew out a breath. "Remind me never to tell you anything ever again."

"Because I'm totally off base? Or because I'm forcing you to confront a difficult truth?"

Damn it, she had him there. Why did he have such perceptive friends?

"All right. You got me. I'm not saying I don't have issues. But I am saying maybe Charlie and I ought to cool off—no pun intended—at least until the arsonist is caught. I can deal with my other suspicions, but that one I need to know for sure."

"You mean *if* he's caught. He eluded the police before, and they still don't have very many leads. You can't pause your life based on vague suspicions and hypotheticals. Spend time with Charlie. Have some fun for once. Accept the fact that a cute, totally normal guy wants to date you. Trust me, it may be difficult for you to believe, but no one else is going to be shocked."

"All right. I'll think about it." He looked up at his ceiling without really seeing anything. "You're a good friend."

"Damn straight I am. You're working the graveyard shift tonight, right?"

"Yup. All by my lonesome too. You'd think being on high alert would mean the other guys would pick up some slack, but nope. Suddenly, they all have dentist appointments and soccer games in the morning."

"To be fair, the arsonist always strikes during the day. Let me know if you want some company."

"Hell no. The chief actually *gave* you a day off. I feel like I'm jinxing it just by saying it out loud. Have a date night with your own cute boyfriend and tell me all the details tomorrow."

"Okay. That actually does sound pretty amazing. Talk to you soon."

"Bye."

Eli ended the call, before lifting his head only to let it drop again. That was apparently the last straw for Moxie, because she shot out of the room. Pistol, on the other hand, rolled over and nearly fell off the mattress. Eli caught him and pulled the cat against his side.

"What am I going to do about this?"

Pistol meowed in response. Eli groped up the cat's spine until he found his head, giving him a scratch behind the ears. "Thanks, buddy. Very wise advice, as always."

A text notification sounded in the quiet room. Eli grabbed his phone and checked it. He'd barely glanced at the screen when the phone slipped out of his grip and dropped right onto his face.

"Ow." He paused to rub his brow before snatching the phone again. It was a text from Charlie.

Hey, gorgeous. I had fun with you the other day. Sorry I didn't get in touch sooner, but I've been swamped. When can I see you again?

He'd ended the text with a smiley face and a rose emoji.

It was adorable, as per usual. Eli felt like he'd been punched in the gut.

Before Eli could think of a response, Chutzpah appeared out of nowhere and batted the phone out of his hand.

"Hey!" Eli leaned over to see where the cat had gone. "Give that back."

Chutzpah had a corner of the case in his mouth and was watching Eli. His posture said he was ready to make a dash for it at the slightest provocation, probably under Eli's bed. If that happened, Eli would have to move the whole thing to get at his cat, and thus his phone. He'd been through that process before with a dead mouse, and it wasn't pleasant.

"Chutzpah," Eli said, making his voice low and sweet. "Give Daddy his phone back."

Chutzpah responded by dropping the phone to the ground, only to bat it around like one of his toys.

Eli sighed. "This is about Charlie, isn't it?"

Chutzpah meowed.

"You want me to go on another date with him, fall in love, and get married, so you can have two dads spoiling you instead of one, right?"

It was all in his head, of course, but he'd swear up and down the cat nodded. Pistol meowed his agreement from his spot on the bed. Eli knew, on some level, that he was projecting his desires onto his cats so he could go on another date with Charlie guilt-free. But hey, the cats didn't need to know that.

"What if I promise to think about it? Then can I have my phone back?"

Rather than respond, Chutzpah simply tore out of the room at top cat speed. Thankfully, he left Eli's phone behind.

"Fucking cats."

Eli rolled to his feet and scooped it off the ground. If he was going to respond, he needed time to think. In the meanwhile, he busied himself around the house. First came the laundry that'd been taunting him all day, followed by a shower. Then he grilled some chicken and made brown rice so he had handy, protein-packed meals ready, one of which he'd take with him tonight. After portioning it out into plastic containers, he wiped down the kitchen counters.

Then, he took a well-deserved nap. He'd need to be well rested if he was going to be up all night fretting. Not simply fretting about his personal life, either. Whoever the arsonist was, he was still out there.

It was strange that he'd set two fires back-to-back and then had gone silent. Before, he'd had a regular schedule. Eli wanted to hope this meant he'd disappeared again, but wasn't that much of an optimist. Chances were, he was going to strike again soon.

Eli was dozing in bed, dreaming about getting up and making himself something to eat before his shift, when his phone went off. The ringtone was the same siren sound their trucks made. It meant the chief was calling. She only did that when there was an emergency.

Sometimes, he hated being right.

"Hello?"

"Johnson." Chief Sappenfield's voice was tight as a bowstring. "There's been another fire. Get to the station and get your gear. Then meet the others on site." She rattled off the location.

Eli knew it well. It was a hospital. A fucking *hospital*. First a school, and now this? Whoever the arsonist was, one thing was for sure: he was a sick fuck.

He sprang to his feet and threw on his uniform over top of the undershirt and boxers he'd been sleeping in, before shoving his feet into work boots. Two minutes later, he burst out his front door and got into his car. As a first responder, he had a special red light for his dash so he could speed without getting pulled over. He turned it on and lay on the gas.

When he arrived at the station, it was unsurprisingly empty, of both people and Dottie III. Once he was in uniform, he'd take one of the utility vehicles to the scene, along with any other stragglers that might've been called in from off duty. Anette would probably show up any minute.

He went straight for the dispatch radio in the glass office. It was also empty. Anyone on the right frequency could respond to an emergency, so it didn't need to be staffed. He tuned it so he could listen to what was happening as he pulled on his turnout gear.

It seemed the fire had started in a dumpster behind St. Mary's Hospital. It'd spread quickly to the other trash receptacles and had blown out several windows in the building itself. The location made it even more of a nightmare than usual. They weren't sure if they needed to evacuate or not, and between biohazards, oxygen tanks, and chemicals, there were so many chances for something to explode.

If the arsonist wanted attention, he was picking excellent ways to get it.

Eli finished getting ready just as Rogers and Anette ran into the station.

"Eli." Anette's eyes were wild as she ran up to him. She was wearing a cocktail dress and heels, which suggested she'd come straight from date night. "Glad to see you haven't left yet."

"No, perfect timing. Where's McPherson?"

"He's already at the scene. He was on duty when the alarm tripped. What's the situation?"

He filled them both in while they dressed. He'd never seen Anette get her gear on so quickly. Rogers was tense all the while. When Eli mentioned possibly evacuating, his face tightened.

"My boy's at that hospital," he said quietly. "Broke a bone at little league. All the kids visited him today to sign his cast."

Eli fought the urge to reach out and squeeze his shoulder. Rogers wouldn't see it as an act of comfort but rather as an assumption of weakness. "Your son's going to be fine, Rogers. Are we waiting on anyone else?"

"No," Anette answered.

"Then let's go."

The drive to the hospital was silent, despite the wail of sirens and the voices constantly crackling over their radios. Anette drove, and through a combination of finesse and a hell of a lead foot, she had them there in no time.

The scene they arrived at was pandemonium. The front of the hospital was lined with emergency vehicles, mostly police cars and fire trucks, since the ambulances and EMS were already where they were supposed to be. That was something.

Walking up, he immediately spotted the chief talking to a paramedic. She caught his eye but didn't stop talking. Merely craned her head toward the back of the hospital. Eli spotted smoke rising above the roof of the building.

He jogged toward it, but instinctively, his eyes swept over the crowds of people around the hospital. He didn't fully comprehend what he was looking for until his brain processed that it wasn't there. Charlie. He was nowhere to be seen. He wasn't at this fire. Thank *Christ*. The relief that flooded through Eli might've been helium, it left him feeling so light and giddy.

Anette and Rogers reached his side, and together, they sprinted around to the back. The offending dumpsters were easy to spot. Flames erupted from their mouths like orange tongues. They were blackened and ringed by halos of char on the building behind them. Eli couldn't tell at a glance which one had been the origin point, but he'd bet on the one second from the middle. The scorch marks there were the biggest.

The street was flooded, undoubtedly from the hoses. It must not have been a chemical fire, or they never would have risked dousing it. Eli found McPherson standing on the far edge with two members of the second crew. They had their extinguishers out and were dousing whatever flames licked their way out of the general containment zone.

At McPherson's shout, Eli joined them. It was grueling, tense work for all that Eli was mostly standing still. The air was thick with heat, and sweat tickled the back of his neck. Every time the fire started to gain ground, they'd beat it back. If Eli allowed himself for a moment to think they'd finally coated the surrounding shrubbery in water, a new blossom of fire would burst up.

It took the better part of an hour, but eventually, the fire was defeated. When the all clear from dispatch went out, a cheer erupted from the fighters ringing the back of the hospital.

Eli found McPherson again in the crowd of masked faces. "Do they know anything yet?"

"No." McPherson flipped his mask down. "There's no investigative report yet, but we're all thinking it: it was probably the arsonist. From what second crew told me, if he'd set the fire a day earlier, before the dumpsters had been emptied for the week, it would have been much worse. This guy's either totally incompetent, or he has terrible luck. His fires never seem to cause any real damage."

Eli's mind was reeling. McPherson might think the arsonist was a joke, but Eli's alternative theory was starting to gain credence. If this was in fact the arsonist's work, then he might be deliberately striking at times when people were unlikely to get hurt. It was still scummy as fuck, but not murderous.

Charlie not being here was a relief, but then again, maybe he'd slipped away before getting caught this time. Eli hadn't responded to his earlier text. What if this was his way of getting a firefighter's attention?

Will you listen to yourself? What kind of egomaniac are you? Thinking this is all about you, when people like Rogers have a serious stake in this. Anette's right: Charlie's a sweet guy who likes you, and you're making something out of nothing. Most importantly, he wasn't here. You said you believed him before. It's time to act like it.

He squashed down the last of his reservations and pulled out his phone. He didn't have time for anything fancy—he was on the job, after all—but he sent Charlie a reply asking how his day was and saying he'd love to see him again. After sending it, he felt a strange sense of peace. He'd made a choice, and now the chips would fall where they may.

With that taken care of, he got to work. Now that the fire was out, it was time for damage control. Mostly, he helped the patients staying in the back rooms get settled into new ones and got aggressively hit on by the lovely women from the geriatrics ward.

After he'd finished helping Mrs. Finkelstein and had declined several invitations to watch *Letterman* with her, he exited the hospital and met up with the chief, who was talking to Anette.

The moment he walked over, she answered the question he hadn't worked up the nerve to ask yet. "They're ninety percent sure it was the arsonist."

Eli cursed violently and then apologized.

"Oh no, use all the colorful language you'd like." She waved him off. "I'd like to tell him to shove some things in some places myself. I hope they catch the bastard this time. It's not looking good, though. I've been talking to the police, and they're clueless."

Eli dithered for only a second before he said, "Chief, have they considered that the arsonist isn't . . ." He struggled for the right words.

"Isn't what?"

"Trying to *hurt* anyone?"

Chief Sappenfield raised an eyebrow at him. "What makes you ask that?"

"All these places . . . A hospital, an elementary school, a grocery store . . . They're so *public*. Either this guy wants to get caught, or he wants attention. I don't think this is about the fires at all."

Gears were ticking behind Chief Sappenfield's eyes. "That's an interesting theory. I don't know how seriously they'll take it without evidence, but I'll pass it along to Detective Thorpe."

"Thank you. If we're all done here, I'm going to head to the station and wait tensely by dispatch."

Anette frowned. "Your shift doesn't start until ten."

"I know, but I'm not going to go there, put away my gear, and go home for a handful of hours only to come back again. I won't be able to relax anyway."

"Fine," the chief said, "but I want you to get some rest. Take a nap on one of the cots. Working the night shift is hard enough when you haven't come straight from a fire. Don't . . ." She paused. "I started to say don't burn yourself out, but that's a little on the nose."

Eli laughed, and some of the tension left his shoulders. "I get what you mean."

Anette piped up. "Well, I, for one, am going to get back into my heels and finish up my date." She looked around for Rogers and waved at him. "You ready to go?"

"I'm going to check on my son," Rogers called back. "Go on without me."

Eli, Anette, and a handful of others got into their truck and headed back to the station. There, they removed, checked, and put away their gear. They had a little laundry room in the back where they could wash their uniforms after a fire, and there was a locker full of unclaimed gear. Eli decided to wash his and use spares in the unlikely chance another fire broke out tonight.

Looking around the station, Eli had never seen so many somber faces before. No one was talking, but everyone seemed to be thinking the same thing. Should they bother putting their gear away? How soon were they going to need it again?

Eli's phone went off in his pocket. Heart racing, he pulled it out. Sure enough, he had a text from Charlie.

What are you up to tonight?

Eli wrote back. *Working. The graveyard shift, sadly.*

When he'd finished, he surveyed the station. Most everyone had filed out as soon as they were done checking their gear. They all had families and lives to get back to, crisis situation or not. Anette shot him a sympathetic look on her way out, but she also had somewhere to be. Someone who was waiting for her. Someone who wasn't feline.

Loneliness hit Eli like a wall as he watched the fire station empty. A few people remained behind—the ones who were finishing out the afternoon shift—but in a couple of hours, they'd be gone too. Once Dottie III returned, the last of them would leave. It'd be him, alone, again.

Eli had a hell of a night ahead of him.

He made his way up to the rec room. With no one in it, it was huge and sort of forlorn. He was about to settle on the couch and sink into some mindless, thought-obliterating TV when his phone buzzed again. Charlie.

Want some company? I could drop by the station and say hi.

Eli's immediate thought was *Hell yeah*, but he tamped that down. Now wasn't an appropriate time to give a tour. They opened the station to the public sometimes, but those were usually fundraising events and field trips. He couldn't invite a civilian here while they were on high alert.

Then again . . . it was unlikely the arsonist would strike twice in one night. It wasn't his MO. Eli would probably spend all of tonight bored and anxious while everyone else got to sleep. Why not enjoy a little harmless company? And on the off chance that they got another call, if Charlie was in Eli's sights at the time, it would prove, beyond any doubt, that he wasn't the arsonist.

Eli debated with himself for a moment longer before crafting a response. *If you were to stop by, emphasis on if, it couldn't be until later. Like, mad later. I don't think bringing a stranger around right now would look good, but I'm working alone tonight, and what they don't know won't hurt them.*

I understand. When does your shift start?

Ten.

Eli waited for a response, but nothing popped up. Not even an ellipsis to indicate typing. After staring at his phone for an unjustifiably long time, Eli slipped it back into his pocket. Maybe ten was too late for Charlie. Maybe he was going to make plans with someone else instead, someone who had time for him and didn't work such demanding hours.

Will you chill the fuck out? Your thirst for this boy is turning you into a needy prom date.

The chief had instructed Eli to rest, but he was too anxious for that. He headed downstairs for a bit. Maybe being social would take his mind off things. Unfortunately, the handful of other people in the station were either volunteers or from the second crew, who had finally returned with a filthy truck they seemed uninterested in cleaning. They weren't anyone he'd spent much time with in the past, and none of them seemed up for chatting.

Eventually, ten o'clock rolled around, and everyone left. Eli stood in the empty fire station, breathing in the smell of diesel and stale smoke, and fought off the blanket of desolation that threatened to wrap around him.

How had he not noticed how empty he'd been lately? What was it about Charlie that highlighted to him how badly he wanted to find someone?

His stomach growled, and it was then that he realized in his haste to get to the scene of the fire, he'd left the food he'd prepared at home. Great. He'd have to order something.

Right on cue, Eli's phone vibrated. And not the usual short notification buzz either. Someone was calling him.

He answered with far too much eagerness. "Hello?"

"I have a riddle for you," Charlie's voice replied. "If I were, say, in the neighborhood of the fire station with far too much Thai takeout and some spare time on my hands, where would I go?"

He's seriously perfect.

Eli's dark mood was dispelled like it'd been blown away. "Hm, that's a tough one. I'd hate for all that food to go to waste. I *suppose* you could bring it here."

"The coast's clear?"

"All clear."

"Great. Be there in five. Bye."

Eli started to say bye back, but then he blurted out, "I can't wait to see you."

Charlie's voice was warm and sincere. "Me neither."

"Bye."

Eli ended the call before he could say anything else embarrassing. One of these days, he'd sit down and examine what it was about Charlie that made him so quick to open up, but for now, he was going to roll with it, enjoy the company, and see what happened.

The garage was closed down for the night, so when Eli got a text from Charlie saying he was in the parking lot, he went out the side door to greet him. The cool night air did nothing to dampen the spark of excitement inside him. A handful of stars were scattered across the charcoal sky, and the moon hung low and heavy, shrouded by wisps of cloud. It was a gorgeous night.

True to his word, Charlie had a brown paper bag that looked like it was about to burst. Eli smelled delicious curry and spices. He wasn't sure which was more mouthwatering: the food or the sight of an adorably rumpled Charlie leaning against a red car.

"Hey, stranger." Charlie grinned at him. A nearby streetlight lit parts of his face while keeping others in shadow. It highlighted his bone structure in the best way.

"Good to see you. You look like you just rolled out of bed." Eli paused a few feet away, unsure if he should go in for a hug or a kiss or what. With a take-out bag between them, any gesture would be difficult to navigate.

Before he could decide, Charlie beat him to it. He took the bag and hefted it against Eli's chest. "I may have taken a nap before I called you. I wanted to be bright-eyed and bushy-tailed for our second date. Do you mind carrying this for me?" He kissed Eli's cheek as he slipped around him. "I'll get the door."

Eli followed him inside, ears ringing with the words *second date*. The warm brush of Charlie's lips lingered on his cheek long after, seeming to promise a hot night ahead.

CHAPTER 6

Charlie had been inside a fire station only once before. He'd been in the second grade, and his class had taken a field trip to one in a more rural part of town. It'd been small, with one truck, one rescue vehicle, and six firefighters who were all dads on the local PTA.

In short, it was nothing like Eli's fire station.

The outside had been suitably impressive, what with the proverbial redbrick and the heavy rescue vehicle parked in front that looked like something out of a survival movie. The inside, however, made Charlie's inner child click his heels together with glee.

His eyes went directly to the pole descending from the ceiling. He'd wondered if those still existed in modern times, and it was a distinct pleasure to discover they did. As his eyes slid over the gleaming cherry-red truck—splattered with mud but still majestic—the lockers, and the tanks that he assumed were filled with water, his excitement only grew.

He walked out into the center of the garage and swept around to face Eli with his arms out. "This place is *awesome*."

Eli, who somehow looked more handsome than ever in his blue Louisville FD shirt, smiled at him indulgently. "I've grown fond of it over the years."

"What's upstairs?"

"The kitchen, rec room, and a storage room where we keep spare equipment. It's got some cots in it for napping during long shifts. And that's where the pole descends from. You want to see it?"

Charlie's head screamed at him to say yes, but he noticed the way Eli was clutching the bag of food to his broad chest like it was a baby. "Let's eat first. I don't know about you, but I'm starving."

"Same. I usually bring something healthy from home to eat, but it's been a long day."

"Hard same. Lead the way."

Eli led him upstairs to a large kitchen with a long wooden table in the center. Charlie could imagine the place full of people in the FD's uniform, sitting at the table, drinking coffee, and waiting to see if they'd be called upon to save lives that day.

"This place has such incredible atmosphere," Charlie said as he took a seat the table. "It feels like something exciting could happen at any moment."

"It's funny you think that." Eli set the bag on the table and pulled containers out of it. "Mostly, we do a lot of waiting around. We clean the trucks, test our equipment, and work out—or at least, some of us do. A few of the older guys seem to think the ten pushups they did back in eighty-seven are sufficient. But beyond that, it's a big waiting game. Though not so much lately."

"I heard there was another fire." Charlie watched Eli's face for any change in expression. "Were you called to it?"

Eli nearly dropped a container of curry. He righted it and stared at Charlie. "How'd you hear about the third fire?"

Charlie furrowed his brow. "Um, the news? Same as everyone else."

"Oh. Right." Eli shook his head. "Sorry. I've been on edge lately."

"I can understand why." He stood up and moved over to Eli's side, leaning a hip against the table next to him. "You're a firefighter, and there's a serial arsonist on the loose. It's like you're Batman, and the Joker is wreaking havoc all over Gotham City."

Eli's lips twitched. "There you go, comparing me to a hero again."

"So what if I am?" Charlie shifted closer, and the scant inches between them filled with heat. "You gonna stop me?" A hint of a dare crept into his tone.

Eli's eyes drifted down to his mouth. "I could. I know a way you might enjoy."

"Oh?" Charlie wet his lips, heart racing. "Show me."

Please kiss me.

Eli was still for a second before he leaned over. Charlie's eyelids dipped down in anticipation of a kiss, but a second later, they flew open again.

Eli had grabbed one of the soft, clear spring rolls and shoved it into Charlie's mouth. "There."

For a second, Charlie was stunned. Then he laughed so hard, he almost spit it out. He managed to bite off the end and swallow so he could giggle without being disgusting. Eli was laughing too, one hand flat on the table as if he needed it to support him.

When Charlie had recovered, he gave Eli a playful shove. "You're lucky I love this place's rolls. That wasn't very nice."

"No," Eli agreed. "But I'm never going to forget your face. I thought your eyes were going to pop out."

"Just for that, I'm not sharing my panang with you. This place makes the best I've ever had."

"What all did you order?"

"A bunch of stuff. I wasn't sure what you'd like, or if you were allergic to anything, or vegetarian."

"Definitely not that last one. I eat a lot of fish."

"Then you should try the scallops." Charlie sifted through the containers until he found the right one. Opening the lid, steam that smelled like butter rose up from half a dozen scallops floating in a delicate sauce.

Eli closed his eyes and moaned. "Oh my God, that smells amazing."

Hesitantly, Charlie reached for one. "May I?"

There was a fraction of a pause, but then Eli's eyes darkened, and he nodded.

Charlie scooped up one of the light-as-air mollusks, shook off the excess sauce, and then maneuvered it toward Eli's parted mouth. Eli did precisely what Charlie's libido had been hoping he'd do. He wrapped his lips around Charlie's fingers and took the scallop with a swirl of tongue that was going to keep Charlie awake at night. Then he made a soft, pleasure-filled sound as he chewed.

Charlie shivered. "Like it?"

"Oh, I liked a lot of things about that." Eli moved closer, pressing Charlie back against the table. "You want a taste?" The intent in his eyes made his meaning clear.

Charlie set the scallops to the side, smiling coyly. "Are you trying to lull me into a false sense of security again? Gonna shove another spring roll into my mouth?"

Eli rested his hands lightly on the table on either side of Charlie's hips. "No tricks this time, I promise." He leaned forward, bringing their bodies together. "Want me to move?"

Charlie was having trouble filling his lungs with air. "If you mean closer, then hell yeah." Having Eli crowded against him felt ridiculously good. He was so solid, and hot in every sense of the word.

"I thought you were hungry," Eli asked, voice rough.

"I am."

Charlie wasn't sure which one of them leaned in first, but suddenly, they were kissing. The moment their mouths touched, Charlie was furious with himself for not making out with Eli as soon as he'd gotten him alone. Eli's lips were every bit as soft as Charlie had imagined they'd be, and he'd been picturing this since the moment they'd met. When Eli made a low noise in his throat and angled his head to deepen the kiss, it was everything Charlie could do to keep his knees from buckling.

The pièce de résistance, however, was when Eli parted his lips and swiped Charlie's with his tongue. Charlie opened up his mouth to him, tasting rich butter sauce. Eli shuffled closer until Charlie's ass was pushed up against the table. The kiss was slow and chaste at the moment, but Charlie felt it shifting to obscene, like a crackle of energy in the air.

Unfortunately, in an attempt to be sexy, Charlie propped a palm on the table with the intention of pressing more firmly against Eli. In so doing, he planted a hand unerringly in a container of rice. He broke the kiss with a snort.

"What—" Eli looked behind him and chuckled. "Very smooth."

"Hush"—Charlie held up his hand—"or prepare to be *riced*." He mimed like he was going to touch Eli's face.

Laughing, Eli grabbed his wrist. They made a show of wrestling—Charlie trying to touch Eli's cheek, and Eli staving him off—but it was clear in seconds that Eli had a serious strength advantage.

By the end of it, they were both giggling so hard they were breathless. Charlie was finally too weak to pretend to fight anymore. He went limp against Eli, resting his head on Eli's shoulder.

Eli semi-carried him to the sink and washed Charlie's hand clean. He smoothed his fingers over Charlie's palm, massaging it.

Charlie's hormones couldn't decide if he was the most relaxed he'd ever been or the most turned on.

"Thank you," he said, surprised to hear how soft his voice was. It was nice to be taken care of, and to have someone who could laugh with him when things went awry.

Eli flashed a smile before shutting off the water, grabbing a dish towel, and patting down his palm. "You're welcome. Ready to eat now?"

"Oh yeah. Nothing can distract me from food for long."

"Good to know."

They spooned various dishes into bowls and ate sitting at the table next to each other, shoulders touching. Eli raved about the food after every mouthful. It was total overkill, but Charlie decided he was fine with it as long as Eli kept making those soft, honeyed sounds between bites. In an effort to hear more of them, Charlie was generous enough to share his panang curry after all.

While they ate, they talked about *everything*. Music. Movies. Their childhoods. Eli was an only child, but Charlie, as he'd mentioned previously, had an older sister. What he'd failed to mention before, however, was something of an awkward subject.

"My parents and I don't really see eye to eye." Charlie took a bite of spicy tofu, tongue stinging pleasantly from the heat. "When my sister and I were growing up, she was definitely the golden child. Made all the best grades, won all the awards, was good at sports. That sort of thing. I was more the sort to wing it and hope for the best."

"I see merit in both approaches."

"Me too. Not my parents, though. They wanted me to buckle down, and the harder they pushed, the more I rebelled. It didn't help that they were constantly comparing me to Kathryn. It got worse when she went off to a great college, met her husband, and got married right after graduation. Now, she has two beautiful children. Meanwhile, I'm still pretty much where I was ten years ago."

Eli nodded. "I get that. Do you resent her?"

"Oh, not at all. It's not her fault our parents like to meddle. I'm totally thrilled for her. She went after what she wanted, and she got it. I've asked her before why she doesn't run for president, and she winks and says she's not thirty-five yet."

"She sounds hilarious, just like you." Eli popped another scallop into his mouth and licked his fingers. "Do you not want any of those things? Marriage and children and all?"

Charlie was briefly mesmerized by the wet flash of Eli's tongue. He had to shake himself away from the memory of Eli sucking on his finger before he could answer. "It's not that I don't *want* them. Someday, I'd love to settle down. I don't think there's any rush, though. My folks want me to have already found someone and bought a house and some diamonds, or whatever it is married people spend their money on. But I'm waiting to do it right. Early thirties are the new early twenties, you know."

"I think waiting to do it right is extremely admirable."

Charlie looked at Eli sidelong. "What about you? You see yourself exercising your constitutional right to marriage?"

"Oh, definitely. I want the full package. A white picket fence. Marriage to the love of my life. A house with a yard. Maybe not kids—I go back and forth on that—but definitely some animals."

"Cats?" Charlie asked.

"I'm open to dogs as well. I don't have the space for one right now, though, since I already have three cats. They're fine indoors, but if I got a dog, I'd want it to have its own space. A yard or a nearby park. I see myself running around and playing with it. Wrestling in the grass on a sunny Sunday afternoon, you know?"

Charlie smiled. "Sounds idyllic. You got a timeframe in mind?"

Eli shook his head. "Not in particular. I'm twenty-eight, and I know to a lot of people, that's past the hump, so to speak, but I'm letting things happen when they happen. I'm like you. I want to make sure I've found my ideal match before I commit for life. I've been in a couple of serious relationships, and I ended all of them."

"You knew they weren't for you each time?"

Eli nodded. "I have pretty good instincts about that. Not always at first, but when I'm a year or so in, I can tell if it's forever or for now."

Charlie abandoned his rice and bumped his shoulder against Eli. "What'd your instincts tell you when we first met?"

"That you're charming. Maybe a little too charming." He grinned and touched their knees together. "And that I like you. Maybe a little too much."

Charlie smiled back and considered going in for more kisses, but he didn't want to end up making out on top of containers of curry. If he got another taste of Eli's lips, that was bound to happen.

Hopping to his feet, Charlie stretched his arms above his head and spun around. "If you're finished eating, how'd you like to give me a tour?"

"A tour? I know what you really want." Eli finished the bite he was eating and got to his feet as well. "You want to see the pole."

Charlie's mind went directly to the gutter, and he had to fish it out before he understood. "Oh my god, really? The fire pole? You'd let me slide down?"

"Sure. You're a grown man. I trust you not to crack your head open. Though, for the record, you're going to watch me do it first." Eli headed for a doorway to the right.

Eyes on his ass, Charlie trailed after. "Gladly."

Eli led him into a spacious storage room with boxes lining the perimeter and a clear path down the middle to the aforementioned pole. Charlie itched to examine the spare air tanks, masks, and sundry supplies stowed away in boxes and shelves, but he didn't want to miss the show.

Looking back at him, Eli took hold of the pole with both hands. "It's easy to do once you get the hang of it. The only tricky part is what to do with your feet. Grab onto it and then lock both feet around it in different directions. Like this."

Eli climbed onto the pole, using his impressive upper-body strength to hold himself in place as he tucked his left leg over the pole, locking in at his ankle, while his right crossed under. He stayed suspended there like it was nothing, biceps bulging. "You got it?"

Charlie's mouth watered, but he nodded. "See you on the other side."

"I'll catch you if you fall." With that, Eli descended, smooth as honey.

Jesus, talk about falling. He's so amazing.

Somehow, it wasn't until Eli's head had disappeared that it occurred to Charlie that he was going to have to do this. No backing down. Shit. He'd been way more comfortable with the *idea* of plummeting down a floor with only a metal pole to stop him from dying.

He squinted down through the hole, which was large enough to accommodate two grown people. Eli was standing at the bottom, grinning up at him and looking far too pleased.

"You're not afraid of heights, are you?" Eli called up.

"No," Charlie lied. "Well . . . maybe a little. Promise you'll catch me?"

"I promise." Eli held out his arms.

I believe him, but my heart's still pounding. I can't wimp out in front of Eli, though. He does this every day.

Charlie took a breath, grabbed the pole in both hands, and sort of hopped onto it. He had no idea if he got his ankles in the right places, because the next thing he knew, he was sliding at what felt like thirty miles an hour. He shrieked all the way down.

A second before he was surely going to plummet through the floor and end up in the molten core of the Earth, warm arms wrapped around him.

Breath tickled his ear. "Gotcha. Told you I'd catch you."

Charlie's feet hit the floor, but he immediately wobbled from a combination of nerves and weak knees. Eli held him tight, turning him around and securing him to his broad chest. The second Charlie looked up, their eyes locked in a way that made Charlie grateful Eli was anchoring him. Otherwise, he was either going to collapse or float up to the ceiling.

"You all right?" Eli smiled. "You did great."

"Thank you, and yeah, I'm fine." He squeezed Eli's forearm. "Thanks for catching me."

"Oh, trust me, it was my pleasure."

The words hung between them, thick with promise. Charlie's heart had already been beating fast, but now it went into overdrive.

"You know," Eli murmured, "all these heart-pounding situations we find ourselves in . . . I think they might be playing with our hormones."

"Maybe." Charlie wet his lip. "Then again, I felt the same when we were having lunch in a quiet deli. I don't need excitement to know I'm into you."

"You swear?" Maybe it was Charlie's imagination, but Eli's face seemed to drift closer.

"Of course." Charlie leaned back against the pole, and Eli came with him. "I know this isn't a toy, but the desire to give you a little striptease is profound."

Eli's hands settled on his hips. "I don't know whether to encourage you or not."

Charlie moved his hips in a slow sway under Eli's hands. "Why not?"

Eli hesitated with his mouth inches from Charlie's. "On one hand, I would *love* to see that. On the other, just thinking about it is making me hot, and I'm at work."

"There's no one here but us." Charlie paused. "Is there something else holding you back? You look pensive."

Eli chewed on his bottom lip, expression growing serious. "I dunno. Call me paranoid, but I've never clicked with someone like this before. I have trouble believing things can be this easy."

He feels it too. It's not in my head. I don't think I dared to believe it.

Charlie had to suck in a breath before he could say, "Don't you think you deserve something easy?"

For some reason, that seemed to spark a fire in Eli. He wrapped his arms around Charlie and kissed him with feeling. Charlie melted into it. The metal bar behind him was far from comfortable, but with Eli warming his front, he hardly cared.

Eli kissed with deliberation. Every press of his mouth was reverent, every flash of teeth or tongue was purposeful. He had Charlie panting against his lips within minutes, and that wasn't even counting what his hands were doing: sliding up and down Charlie's sides, stopping to graze a hip bone or squeeze his waist possessively.

Charlie tried to keep it together. He really did. But Eli fit against him like they'd been designed for this, and with him kissing Charlie with such raw intent, it was impossible not to respond. Quickly, Charlie got hard.

He started to back off, unsure of how Eli would react to his . . . enthusiasm. They'd only known each other for a week, after all. But when he shifted, Eli moved with him, widening his stance and pressing their hips together. God, they fit together so well. Charlie broke their kiss and gasped at the feel of answering hardness between Eli's legs.

Eli kissed up his neck and found his ear. "Is this okay?"

Charlie tried to form words but ended up making some sort of half affirmation, half moan.

Chuckling against his skin, Eli nipped his earlobe. "I'll take that as a yes." Without warning, Eli scooped Charlie up under the thighs and lifted him like he weighed nothing.

Charlie let out an embarrassingly heated groan and wrapped his legs around Eli. He slipped his arms around Eli's neck and pulled him in for a hot, open-mouthed kiss. With their groins together—nothing between them but clothes that were clinging with sweat—kissing was so much more intense.

An itch was building in Charlie, a deeper need that begged to be satisfied. Pretty soon, kissing wasn't going to be enough. He needed to find out if he and Eli were on the same page before he got too worked up. He was pretty sure they were—he could feel how into him Eli was every time he canted his hips—but he wanted confirmation.

"Fun as this is," Charlie said between kisses, "the pole is starting to dig into my spine."

"Sorry." Eli mouthed his throat, not sounding the tiniest bit sorry. "What do you want to do? Stop? We probably should, since I'm working and all."

"No. Fuck no." Charlie was so turned on, he felt dizzy. He sucked in a breath. "There are those cots upstairs."

"Too far."

Suddenly, they were moving. Or rather, Eli was carrying Charlie. Charlie didn't look to see where they were going. Looking would mean not kissing Eli anymore, and he certainly didn't want that.

A second later, his back hit cool metal. Eli must've carried him to the lockers he'd seen on his way in. With a proper flat surface behind Charlie, Eli was able to press their bodies together in earnest, and then he ground his hips. Charlie couldn't stop a sweet moan from pouring out of him, and Eli reacted by rutting harder against him. Everything was hot and damp and much, much too raw, but Charlie couldn't seem to get enough.

"Are you sure you're all right with this?" Charlie hated to ask, but it was the responsible thing to do. "I know you said you're working alone tonight, but we're still sort of out in the open."

That was technically true, but tucked off to the side like this, if someone walked in through the side door Charlie had entered, they wouldn't see them right away.

That's not the same thing as being somewhere private, though, he debated with himself.

A second later, Eli shook his head. "Everyone's exhausted from being on high alert. The only way anyone will show up here is if there's an alarm, and if that happens, I'm sorry, but I'll straight up kick you out." He nipped playfully at Charlie's chin. "I hope that's okay. I appreciate you asking."

"It's fine by me. I get it." Charlie took Eli's face in both hands and planted a firm kiss on his lips. "I was hoping you wouldn't want to stop."

"Far from it. If you ask me, you have on too much clothing." He set Charlie down so he could push his shirt up and run blunt fingernails down his stomach. Charlie shivered at the sharp sensation and flexed on instinct. He was nowhere near as cut as Eli, but Eli whistled appreciatively.

He pushed Charlie's shirt up a bit more and paused. "What's this?" The bottom of a gray design was visible.

Charlie sucked in air so he could answer. "I told you that if you were lucky, I'd show you my tattoo."

"Wow, I'd forgotten. Is it a constellation?" A smattering of different-sized stars were scattered on the left side of his stomach, above his hip bone. "Do they mean something?"

"It's my version of a family tree. The two big stars are my parents, the medium one is my sister, and the little ones are my niece and nephew. Someday, if I have kids, I'll add more." His face heated. "Sorry, I know it's not sexy to talk about family when we're fooling around."

"On the contrary, I think it's endearing. And *very* sexy." He nuzzled Charlie's neck. "It's something else we have in common too: we both have family tattoos."

"I like that." Charlie scraped his nails lightly down the back of Eli's neck. "I liked it better when you were undressing me, though."

Eli made a low, wanting sound. As Charlie watched, his limbs trembling, Eli's hand dipped lower to his fly. Eli paused shy of touching the bulge that'd formed in the front of Charlie's jeans. He spoke in an undertone. "What do you want me to do?"

"Whatever you want." Charlie skimmed his lips along Eli's strong jawline. "So far, everything's felt amazing. I trust you. I'll take whatever you give me."

At that, a deep rumble sounded from Eli's chest, almost like a purr. "So sexy. C'mere." Charlie hadn't thought it was possible for them to get closer, but Eli fitted an arm in the small of Charlie's back and held him tight. With his free hand, he undid Charlie's fly.

Charlie started to reach down to help him, but Eli had his button undone and zipper down before he could.

He moaned. "Holy shit, that's hot."

"Comes from years of having to assemble gear quickly." Eli's mouth was at his ear again, his breath soft and tickling. "Speaking of hot." Eli's fingers slipped into Charlie's underwear.

Charlie thought he'd prepared himself for what it would feel like to have Eli touch his cock, but he couldn't have been more wrong. Eli's hands were rough in the best way, and when he stroked the length of Charlie from head to base, pleasure burst between his legs.

"Fuck." Charlie grabbed Eli's shoulders, feeling weak. "So good. Don't stop."

Eli nuzzled his neck while he palmed him, slow but steady. Charlie was caught between wanting to beg him to go faster and knowing he'd come on the spot if Eli did. Through a heady haze of arousal, it occurred to him that he should be returning the favor. His mouth watered at the idea of seeing Eli's dick. The desire was strong enough to lift him from the pleasured stupor Eli was sinking him into.

He shoved a hand between their bodies and rubbed Eli through his pants. He felt more than heard the low groan that rippled through Eli. It took some fumbling—Eli never stopped stroking him all the while, which made concentration impossible—but Charlie managed to get Eli's pants open and his cock out as well.

They stood there for a moment, both panting and staring down at themselves. Eli's hand wrapped around Charlie's ruddy cock was a gorgeous mirror to Charlie holding Eli's darker one.

Charlie looked up, a question in his eyes. Eli met his gaze from inches away.

"I don't have anything on me," Eli said.

Charlie instantly understood what he meant. He hadn't come prepared either: no lube or condoms to speak of. He hadn't exactly planned this, though to be honest, considering how his body usually reacted to Eli, he should've had more foresight.

But he didn't care how they got off, so long as he got to be with Eli.

"This is more than fine," Charlie replied. "I already feel like I'm going to burst."

The mood shifted from urgent to intimate in a flash. Their breaths mingled as they both seemed to get the same idea at the same time. Charlie started moving his hand. Eli followed suit, matching his rhythm.

They were quiet as they jacked each other off, only their labored breathing breaking the silence. At least, at first. On an uptick, Eli gave Charlie's head a squeeze, and Charlie whimpered. The sound was loud and embarrassing in the silence, but then he mimicked the motion on Eli, pulling a moan from him.

In this way, Eli guided Charlie through pleasuring him. When he sped up, Charlie did the same. If he tried something, Charlie would try it back. Anything that earned a good reaction got put on a repeat list, and soon, they were both moaning steadily.

Eli's arm was still bracing Charlie's back, but now it seemed to be for his benefit as well, as if he were gripping onto Charlie to keep from flying apart.

Through gritted teeth, he said, "I'm close. So close. Are you?"

Charlie could only nod. He'd been close since they'd been making out. He'd only been holding it together through a sheer desire not to orgasm too soon the first time they did this. "Breathe on me the right way, and I'll come."

"Go ahead." Eli's eyes were bottomless with desire. "I want to see it. Come all over—"

One look at him, and Charlie fell apart. More like shattered. He shuddered through an orgasm he'd known was coming, and yet he still managed to be utterly surprised by the intensity of it. He could hear himself crying out, thick and rich, but he couldn't feel anything outside of the pleasure reverberating through him.

Eli held him through it, thank God, but a second later, Eli shouted, and then he came too. He stiffened, eyes shut, and his tortured expression was so beautiful it was painful to look at.

They slid to the floor together, neither seeming to have the strength to support themselves. Eli ended up on his knees between Charlie's outstretched legs, while Charlie's head lolled back against the lockers. The cool metal felt good against his over-hot skin.

Several deep breaths later, his head cleared. He blinked, and it was like the world came back into focus. His clothes were a mess, as was his hand, but satisfaction had sunk into his bones. He couldn't bring himself to care about his appearance. Eli was still panting for breath, chin lifted up toward the ceiling. He was a vision with his pants undone, his semihard cock still out, and his hair damp with sweat.

Charlie tried to say something but ended up grunting.

Eli nodded. "Same." He wobbled to his feet. "Hold on a sec." He turned around and opened one of the lockers.

Charlie tried to watch what he was doing, but his eyes were sliding closed. He heard a papery sound—tissues?—and some rustling. Then the metallic *click* of the locker being shut. Next thing he knew, something was pressed into his hand.

"Here, clean up with this."

Charlie forced his eyes open. Eli had cleaned up and tucked himself away. He had a packet of tissues open.

"I can't," Charlie joked. "I'm too tired."

To his surprise, Eli grabbed another tissue and started wiping him with care.

Charlie sat up. "Wait, you don't have to do that. I was kidding."

Eli shushed him and kept mopping up. The tenderness with which he did it stirred something in Charlie's hormone-drenched body. The same sort of safe, protected feeling he'd had when Eli had ordered him out of the deli, or when he'd insisted on checking Charlie's breathing, despite all his protests.

As Eli took care of him, Charlie was filled with a desire that went deeper than lust. He wasn't entirely certain what it was until Eli tucked him away, fixed his clothes, and smiled at him. "There, all better."

"Come to my house," Charlie blurted out. "Let me make you dinner."

Eli startled and looked up, wide-eyed like a deer. "Uh, right now? I'm still pretty full from the Thai food."

"No, sometime this week. Whenever you're free. You do so much, not only for me, but in general. I want to do something for you." He shifted. "If you want to see me again, that is."

"Hm, let me think about that." Eli tapped his chin. "*Hell* yeah. Of course I do."

Charlie hadn't had any real doubts, but he still warmed at hearing it. "Really?"

"A resounding yes to that. I'll admit, in the beginning, I had some hesitations . . . but screw it. I like you. I want to see you again. I'm going to go with the flow for once and let things happen."

At that, Charlie felt a twinge of guilt. He wasn't being totally honest with Eli, and here Eli was, taking a chance on him.

You'll tell him eventually, he assured himself. *Dodge him for a little bit longer, until you get a read on how he's going to react to your secret. In the meanwhile, this is your chance to win him over.*

"Can I trouble you for a hand up?" Charlie asked.

Eli bent down and held out a palm. Charlie took it, and Eli hauled him easily to his feet. Had Charlie not had an earth-shattering orgasm moments before, that might've gotten him going again.

"Be honest, do you think you could bench-press me?"

"You'd be better off asking how many reps I could do." Eli winked. "I dunno about you, but that tuckered me out. I think I'll take a nap so I'll be alert if we get a call."

"In that case, I'll leave you to it."

"You don't have to go."

"I know, but I should. I feel guilty for using up your energy." He grinned. "And for defiling your workplace."

"You say 'defiling.' I say 'improving.'" Eli kissed him chastely on the mouth. "Can I convince you to let me send you home with leftovers?"

"Nope, that food is all yours. Refuel, and get ready to have your mind blown when I cook for you. I'll text you tomorrow, and we'll pick a date. Okay?"

"Okay."

Eli escorted him out. As Charlie headed for his car, the expression "walking on air" drifted into his mind. Right before he climbed into the driver's seat, he glanced back at the station and found Eli watching him from the side door. Their eyes met, and even from a distance, Eli's final smile before he disappeared inside was dazzling.

I could fall for him so easily. Charlie's chest tightened. *God, I hope this all works out.*

CHAPTER 7

Thanks to his tight schedule, Eli wasn't able to plan a get-together with Charlie until the following weekend. As it currently stood, on Friday, Eli would go over to Charlie's place, and Charlie would cook. Charlie hadn't told him what he planned to make, but he'd quizzed Eli on his food preferences, allergies, and how much spice Eli could handle. Eli was certain he was in for a culinary journey.

In the meantime, they texted practically every minute of the day. Jokes. Pictures of their lunch. Little work gripes. Everything.

On Thursday evening, when Eli was once again bored and alone in the fire station, and their date was a mere day away, he sent Charlie a picture of himself lounging against the firefighter's pole with his shirt rucked up above his defined stomach. *That* earned him a dozen heart emojis and a lying-in-bed selfie of Charlie biting his lip, eyes dark with hunger. Eli immediately made it Charlie's contact photo.

All in all, everything was going well. Eli was riding the new-relationship high, and Charlie was pretty much everything he'd been searching for.

Except for one small problem.

Charlie was still evasive about certain topics. Not simply his alleged boring office job, but where he'd gone to school, what he'd studied, and what his plans for the future were. These were questions Eli asked every potential partner. It was important to know that their goals and ambitions lined up. But Charlie kept brushing him off, usually with a joke response or a subtle change of topic.

Eli was letting it go, for now. It was still early enough that he didn't feel the need to know where Charlie saw himself in five years. But eventually, Charlie was either going to have to open up on his own, or Eli would have to confront him. He wasn't looking forward to that conversation, because if Charlie really was dodging him on purpose, there had to be a reason, and Eli had a sneaking suspicion he already knew what it was.

But right now, he was happy to bask in the golden glow of infatuation.

By the time Friday rolled around, he was so impatient, he felt like he was going to fly out of his skin. Anette noticed his jitters and pulled him aside at the end of their shift to ask what was up.

"I have a date with Charlie tonight," Eli said as they stood by their respective lockers, packing away their gear. He explained their plans, trying not to let too much excitement drip into his tone.

"That's great!" Anette had a devilish grin on her face. "I was hoping you'd decide to see him. So, are you over your whole thing where you thought he might be the—"

"Shhh!" Eli glanced around. No one was paying attention to them, but the station was still packed. Anyone could overhear them. "Don't say it. But yeah, I'm over it. I'll feel better when we catch the guy, but you were right. It was silly of me to jump to conclusions. Though I still think he's up to something shady, and if that's the case, I'm going to have a tough decision to make."

"You said you're having dinner at his place, right? Think this date's going to be an overnight thing?"

Eli's face warmed. Unbidden, the memory of getting off with Charlie popped into his head, as it had every time he'd glanced at the lockers all week. It'd made its way into more than one of his recent daydreams. If Charlie was up for a repeat performance, then Eli sure as hell was too.

"I don't know," he said. "Maybe. It might be a little soon for that, though."

"It's been a couple of weeks, hasn't it?" She used the mirror inside her locker to pin her voluminous hair back with bobby pins. "I know he's the one you've been texting every spare minute from the goofy smile that never leaves your face. Plus, you already know he's funny and family-oriented and ready to run into a burning building if needed. Sounds to me like you should be dropping the *b* word any day now."

Eli crinkled his brow. "Bottom?"

Anette fumbled a bobby pin and had to brace herself against the locker, she was laughing so hard. "Oh my God, one-track mind much?"

"Guilty as charged." Eli shrugged. "I take it you meant 'boyfriend.'"

"Yeah, smart-ass. Although, that straight up made my day."

"I guess we'll see how this date goes. I'm happy to take my time though, and Charlie is too. We both want—"

"To do things right," she finished. "I know, and I respect that. Not wanting to move too fast and mess up a good thing is perfectly understandable. But make sure you're not pumping the brakes too hard. I don't think Charlie's gonna wait around for you to get on his level. From what you've told me, he sounds like he's ready to go."

"Yeah, true. I promise I'll keep that in mind."

They finished packing up, waved to Chief Sappenfield—who basically lived in the dispatch office these days, waiting for news of the arsonist—and headed out. With a final goodbye, they parted ways to walk to their separate cars.

Eli drove home and fed the cats, like he always did. Then, after consulting with his ever-opinionated aunties for a full half an hour, he changed into approved date-with-a-white-boy clothes: nice well-worn jeans and a black polo shirt. He went through his entire morning grooming routine again. When he'd shaved and had minty-fresh breath, he ran some shea butter through his tight curls, which made his long-on-the-top hair springy and soft. More importantly, it smelled *amazing*.

Checking himself out in the bathroom mirror, he thought he looked pretty damn good. This was more effort than he'd put into an outfit in a long time, and it gave him much-needed confidence. The day before, he'd picked up a bottle of red wine for the occasion and everything. He didn't even like wine, but Charlie had assured him it would go wonderfully with dinner.

He checked the time on his phone. His shift had ended at seven, and it was a little after eight now. Charlie had told him to come over whenever he was ready.

Eli shot him a quick text. *On my way, and I'm bringing an appetite.*

As soon as he sent it, what Anette had said about spending the night popped into his head and gave the text all new meaning. His face heated up again. At this rate, he was going to need an ice pack.

His phone pinged. Charlie had texted back.

Excellent. There's plenty of food. Can't wait to see you.

Eli hesitated for only a second before writing back, *Same.* Then he added a rose emoji, which had become their own personal meme. Except Eli doubted this one was going to get old.

The drive was easy and uneventful. Charlie lived fifteen minutes away, in a more urban area. Instead of the quiet, house-lined street that Eli lived on, Charlie rented an apartment in a big complex, surrounded by shops and restaurants. It was the sort of place Eli would have loved back in college, before he'd had a bedtime and bills to pay. At least Charlie's unit was tucked into the corner. That gave it a semblance of peace and quiet.

The second he knocked on the door, it opened. Charlie's smiling face appeared in the doorway. He was barefoot in loose sweatpants and a tight tank top. Eli instantly felt overdressed, but the whole ready-for-bed look worked on Charlie. And on Eli, in a different way.

"So glad you could make it." Charlie stepped forward, gave Eli a quick but firm kiss, and then opened the door wider, gesturing for him to come in. "Dinner's almost ready."

The smell hit Eli before the door had closed behind him. Butter, spices, and the sharp, salty aroma of bacon. "Oh my God, my mouth is watering. What is that?"

"Come see." Charlie took the wine from him before holding his hand in a loose grip and leading him into the apartment.

It was clean. Like, suspiciously clean. Wiped-crime-scene clean. There were piles of books and folders that suggested his place was usually a lot messier. Eli smiled at the thought that Charlie had gone out of his way to make a good first impression, and that he hadn't quite masked all the evidence.

He tugged Eli into a small kitchen. On the stove, a pot of water boiled next to a pan where a delicious-looking creamy sauce simmered gently.

"*Et voilà!*" Charlie waved at the stove like he was showing off a prize on a gameshow. "Homemade carbonara sauce, and I'm about to make the fettucine. It's gotta go in the pot for a few minutes—long enough to get tender—and then it's ready."

Eli spotted a pasta-maker on the countertop. "Wow, you went all out. When you said you love to cook, you weren't kidding."

"I do, but I'm also showing off a little. I wanted to make you something nice." Charlie grabbed a spoon off a rest, dipped it into the sauce, and cupped a hand under it as he raised it up to Eli. "Try?"

Eli opened his mouth and moaned as soon as the sauce hit his tongue. It was salty, creamy, and had perfect notes of garlic, smoke from the bacon, and parmesan. "Fuck, that's good."

"I'm glad." Charlie tossed the spoon into the nearby sink before turning back to him. "Want a glass of wine while I finish up?"

"Yeah, but let me pour for us. You've done plenty."

Charlie pointed him to a corkscrew and some long-stemmed glasses. After uncorking it, Eli let the wine breathe for a few minutes before pouring. He'd read you were supposed to do that somewhere. It also afforded him an opportunity to watch Charlie cook.

Charlie sprinkled flour over the dough he'd made for the noodles before feeding it into the pasta maker, humming all the while. It was adorably domestic.

When he'd finished, he dumped the fresh noodles into the water, turned off the heat, and accepted the glass of wine Eli handed to him. "Should be ready in a minute." He sniffed the wine. "Mmm, this is going to be perfect with the sauce."

"You know anything about wine?" Eli asked.

"A bit. Not enough to impress at a swanky party. I know red wine goes well with fatty foods, like steaks and rich sauces. Something about tannins and whatnot. You?"

"No, I'm not much of a drinker. Occupational hazard."

"Makes sense. When you could get called in at any hour, you wouldn't want to crack open a bottle of wine at the end of a long day." Charlie took a sip and nodded. "Yup, this is perfect. Want to have a seat while I finish up?" He gestured to the living room across from the kitchen.

Eli wandered over. His eyes were drawn to an artsy corkboard above the sofa. On it, photos of what he assumed were Charlie's family had been mounted with colorful pushpins. They all had his bright, easy smile. Eli would bet they were one of those families who actually had fun when they got together for Thanksgiving and birthdays.

"Are these your parents?" Eli called toward the kitchen, pointing to a picture in the corner of a man and woman standing in front of a prim little house.

Charlie peered over. "Yup. That's Mary Ann and Patrick, or as I know them, Mom and Dad. They bought a condo last year in Clarksville, just north of here, so it's really easy for us to get together. Like when I have lunch with my mom once a week."

"I remember you mentioning that at lunch." Eli hesitated. "That's the second time I've heard the name Mary Ann recently."

Charlie hopped onto the counter next to the stove—one eye on his simmering sauce—and took a sip of wine. "Oh?"

"Yeah. Not to bring up a grim topic, but did you follow the first string of fires from three years ago at all?"

"They were hard to miss. The press had a field day."

"I remember. Somehow it got out that Billy Ray Phelan had been brought in for questioning, and within days, the news was everywhere. Reporters all but said Billy was guilty. It didn't matter how many statements to the contrary the police released. All those old Southern tongues were already wagging."

"Especially after that one Channel 8 segment with Peter Lester went viral." Charlie scrunched his nose. "It was fucking shameful. Everyone called it investigative journalism, but it was just high-end gossip. Poor Billy. Whatever happened to him?"

"I heard he moved across the country. Got away from all the nastiness and started over."

"Good." Charlie climbed off the counter and gave the noodles a stir before turning back to Eli. "What's all this got to do with my mom, though?"

"Billy's mom was also named Mary Ann. She came down to the station a while ago to basically threaten Chief Sappenfield. Told all of us to stay away from her family. It doesn't make a whole lot of sense, considering these fires are a good thing for her son, but she was spittin' mad. Called the chief a dirty Mexican."

Charlie flinched. "Shit. My mom will go straight up Terminator on someone for messing with her kids, but that's not okay."

"You're really close with your family, aren't you?"

"Yeah, including the one I cobbled together for myself here in Louisville. Like my buddy Amos. You'd like him. Or at least, you'd better, because he's my best friend."

"With a name like Amos, he's either Jewish or black." Eli cocked his head. "Or both, I suppose."

"He's black, and too irreverent to be religious."

Eli smiled. "So, if we don't get along, I'm out?"

"Pretty much, yeah." Charlie winked. "Sorry, but he was here first. You got anyone like that?"

"Anette. You met her briefly at the elementary school. But I don't think you have anything to worry about. She already likes you."

"I remember her. She said our meeting was fate."

Eli fought back a grin. "She believes in that sort of thing, like the others."

"Maybe I'll make a believer out of you someday." Charlie grabbed two plates. He piled them with food, and then held up his steaming creations. "You ready to eat?"

"Oh yeah. Could not be more excited about this."

They sat next to each other at the table, knees touching, and ate what was easily the best pasta Eli had ever had outside of a restaurant. He raved about it so much, Charlie actually blushed. When he'd finished embarrassing Charlie, they chatted between bites. Eli was delighted to discover they weren't about to run out of topics anytime soon. Charlie was as easy to talk to as ever. Funny, insightful, and a great listener.

After, they cuddled up on the couch and watched a movie. Eli was grateful Charlie had gone easy on the garlic, because they barely made it ten minutes in before they were making out. It wasn't heated; at least, not overtly. Neither of them seemed to be in any rush to move after their big meal. Charlie had leaned against Eli's chest, and Eli hadn't been able to stop himself from nosing his hair and nipping at his ear. Naturally, that had led to kissing, slow and languid.

At some point, they'd ended up reclining together in a tangle of limbs. The couch was soft and easy to sink into, and with Charlie's warm weight beside him, Eli found himself nodding off.

The next thing he knew, sunlight was warming his eyelids. He cracked one eye open and blinked his gaze into focus. For a split second, he couldn't remember where he was. Then Charlie shifted against him, and he remembered.

Charlie's face was captivating in sleep: so peaceful. Long eyelashes left dark shadows on his cheeks. His lips were parted slightly, still a little kiss-swollen from the night before. One hand was flat against Eli's chest, as if he'd wanted to hold on to him.

It'd be such a shame to wake him, but Eli needed to find a bathroom. As gently as he could, he eased himself off the couch. He expected Charlie to wake up, but he must've been a hell of a heavy sleeper. He barely stirred as Eli moved a pillow under his head and slipped away.

Eli checked out two doors in the entryway that he hadn't noticed the night before. One led to a neat bedroom decorated in soft blues and grays, while the other yielded the sought-after bathroom. He hurried through a miniature version of his morning routine and even found some minty mouthwash to get the taste of last night's wine off his tongue.

When he'd finished, he tiptoed back out to the living room. He considered going into the kitchen and seeing if he could work Charlie's coffeepot, but he didn't want to risk making any noise. Charlie was still sleeping, looking casually gorgeous with his tank top rumpled and a strip of his stomach peeking out above his sweatpants.

The sight struck Eli, and it took him a moment to figure out why. They'd hit a milestone without even trying. They'd spent the night together. And it hadn't been about sex, either. This had been pure comfort and companionship. Having that this early in the relationship, when they should be all lust and hormones, had to mean something big. Didn't it?

Spurred on, Eli kneeled next to the couch and kissed Charlie awake. Charlie's lips were soft and sleep-warm. For a second, he didn't respond. Then, he kissed back, making a rumbling noise in his throat. Eli had only intended to give him a quick peck, but as he started to pull away, Charlie fisted a hand in his shirt, holding him in place.

"Morning," Charlie murmured, mouth brushing against Eli's. His voice was rough with sleep and something else that made Eli's cock perk up.

"Morning," Eli said back, trying to get a read on Charlie's mood.

It became a hell of a lot clearer when Charlie tugged him forward. "Come back to bed."

Eli didn't need to be told twice. He climbed onto the couch, ready to scoop Charlie into his arms and have a lazy morning make-out session. To his surprise, Charlie was much more purposeful than he'd been the night before. His arms went around Eli's shoulders and held on tight. When Eli climbed on top of him, he spread his thighs, allowing their bodies to fit together just right. He kissed with eagerness that made Eli's nerve endings sing.

There wasn't as much room on the couch as there would have been in a bed, and they were both a little musky after sleeping in their clothes, but Eli couldn't have cared less. It was like being with Charlie filled his veins with liquid fire.

Any small thing could get him going, like when Charlie scraped his stubbly jaw down Eli's throat. Eli cursed under his breath, already hard. He was about to back off when Charlie rocked his pelvis against him. His erection was prominent through his clothing. He moaned and squeezed Eli tighter when their dicks lined up and rubbed together.

It never ceased to amaze Eli how quickly things could become hot and intense between them. One second, they were kissing and half-heartedly fooling around. The next, Charlie was biting his neck and attacking his jeans like they'd explode if he didn't get them off right then.

"Want you so bad," Charlie murmured against Eli's skin, skimming his lips along Eli's jawline. "Wanted you last night. Fucking sleep."

"I'm glad we didn't do anything last night," Eli said. Charlie got his pants undone. Eli had to bite back a moan as eager hands slid into his underwear. "That said, I'm *really* happy to be doing this now."

He reached for Charlie's pants and returned the favor. It took some maneuvering in the small space, but eventually he had Charlie's sweats shoved down to his thighs along with his underwear, freeing his cock. At the first touch of Eli's hand to it, Charlie shuddered.

The reaction did more for Eli than Charlie's fingers curling around him. Charlie's eyes fluttered closed, and he made the smallest, sexiest sound. Suddenly, Eli didn't just want sex. He wanted to fuck Charlie. *Now.*

"Charlie." Eli kissed the name into the long column of Charlie's throat. "What do you want to do?" After last time at the station, Eli had come prepared. He had a fresh condom in his wallet, ready to go. Charlie might have other plans, though.

"Let's relocate." Charlie shivered under him and got harder in Eli's hand. "I have supplies in the bedroom. Give me a minute to freshen up, and then I want you to fuck me."

"Oh, thank *God.*" Eli hummed his approval against Charlie's skin. "I was hoping you'd say that."

He hauled Charlie up and then practically raced to the bedroom he'd found earlier. Charlie laughed and followed behind him, stopping off at the bathroom. When he emerged a few minutes later, he had minty breath and looked like he'd splashed some water on his face. He'd left the scruff darkening his jaw, though. Eli would have to send him a thank-you card later.

Charlie rooted around in a drawer before dumping a bottle of lube and an ambitious number of condoms onto the bed. Then he wrapped his arms around Eli and kissed him, hot and wet.

Eli paused long enough to pull his shirt off before he eased Charlie back onto the bed. Charlie wriggled out of his clothing with impressive speed, leaving him deliciously naked. Rubbing bare skin to bare skin was almost as good as the feel of Charlie's hard cock nestled against his thigh.

It became apparent the second Eli started touching Charlie that he was vocal in bed. Every brush of his fingers wrung a desperate noise from him. Eli had a feeling he was going to hear Charlie's honeyed moans ringing in his ears for a long while.

Eli was reaching for the lube when Charlie angled his hips so their dicks slid perfectly together, heavy and velvety soft. Eli lost his concentration for a solid minute while he rutted against Charlie until they were both sweaty and quivering.

"Eli," Charlie said, voice raw with desire, "if you don't fuck me soon, I'm going to die."

Eli huffed a breath and reached for the lube once more. "It'd help if you'd stop wriggling."

"I caaan't. It feels too good." Despite the protest, his hips finally stilled.

Eli seized the opportunity. He lubed up two fingers, eased Charlie's thighs apart, and began preparing him. Charlie worked with him, keeping relaxed and moving with Eli's rhythm as he got two slick fingers into him, followed shortly by a third.

By the time Charlie was properly stretched, he was panting and flushed. The sight of him alone had been enough to keep Eli unflaggingly hard throughout the process.

He removed his fingers and kneeled between Charlie's legs. "You ready?"

Charlie nodded, licking his lips. He was watching Eli from beneath lowered eyelids. "Been ready."

Eli got a condom, rolled it on, and took himself in hand. It was far from the most thorough job he'd ever done preparing someone, but when he pressed into Charlie, he slid right home, like Charlie's body wanted him there. It felt *incredible*.

"Fuck." He shuddered and stilled as sensations lapped over him. "Wasn't expecting that."

Charlie grunted but didn't speak. Beneath Eli, he adjusted his position, getting comfortable. The motion made Eli hiss, but he held it together while Charlie found what worked for him, spreading his legs wider and angling up his hips.

When Charlie had finished, he slipped his arms around Eli's neck and kissed Eli's chin. "Move."

The permission shattered the last of Eli's self-restraint. He set a quick, deep rhythm that wrung moans from them both. Charlie held on to him, fingers digging bluntly into his shoulders. Eli kept an ear out for signs of pain, but all Charlie did was moan and stammer a variety of encouragements.

Within minutes, the pleasure inside of Eli began to tighten like a spring. Charlie was clenching around him, and with his sweet voice in Eli's ear, there was no stopping the arousal building up in him. He pulled together enough self-awareness to slide a hand between their bodies and find Charlie's cock. The moment he did, Charlie seized up.

Eli paused. "You okay?"

Charlie nodded, eyes clenched shut. "I didn't realize how close I was. I— Oh *fuck*, Eli."

Eli had started stroking him. Charlie's long, deep rumble of desire spurred him on. Eli was right on the edge as well, and Charlie's pleasure was resonating through him as sure as if he were feeling it too.

When Charlie hooked a leg around him—heel digging into the small of Eli's back, drawing him in deeper—Eli lost it. He fucked Charlie hard and fast, barely managing to pump his cock between punishing thrusts.

Charlie came with a garbled shout, spilling all over Eli's hand and his own stomach. Eli tumbled after him a second later. His mouth found Charlie's, and he shuddered out a moan against his sweat-salty skin. When he was spent, his muscles gave out, rolling him onto his side.

It took him several minutes of deep breathing to come down, and even then, he felt foggy with hormones. The kind he hadn't felt since he was a teenager having sex for the first time. The kind that made him feel drunk and giddy. The dangerous kind.

"Holy shit, that was awesome," Charlie slurred. He'd collapsed against the bed in a sprawl, but now he was pawing at Eli. "C'mere."

Eli pushed himself up on shaky arms and crawled to Charlie's side. He paused long enough to toss the condom in the bedside trash before he dissolved, pulse still pounding. Charlie pulled him close so his head was on Charlie's chest. His audible heartbeat was every bit as wild.

Charlie buried his face in Eli's hair and breathed deep. "You smell good. Like coconut or something."

"It's shea butter," Eli said, tongue thick. "Gotta keep my hair all luxurious."

He both heard and felt Charlie's soft chuckle. "We just woke up, and I could already take a nap."

"Well, you've been busy." Eli angled his head up for a kiss. "I have a shift later, or I'd be down for a nap. Maybe in a minute, I'll get up and make you breakfast. You earned it."

"Don't go." Charlie tightened his arms around him. "To work, I mean. I miss you when you're not around."

"I miss you too."

Goddamn. Eli was so drunk on postcoital satisfaction, he actually considered calling out. While an arsonist was running loose. What was the matter with him?

This was what he meant when he'd called this dangerous. Good sex could trick you into feeling things, like something suspiciously close to love, when it was *way* too soon for that.

But in this case . . . if it was for Charlie . . . was that really such a bad thing?

"Can I ask you something?" Eli said.

Charlie nodded, smoothing his fingers down Eli's sweaty back.

"Do you think this is . . . going *too* well?"

Charlie startled a little and leaned back to look him in the eye. "What? You say that like it's a bad thing. I'm a big fan of things going well."

"Right, of course. What I meant was . . . I'm not sure. Things seem like they're moving at lightning speed."

Charlie sat up, which forced Eli to prop himself on an elbow. "You picked a hell of a time to tell me you want to pump the brakes."

"I don't. I swear." Eli waved his free hand. "That's not what I'm saying. Actually, I don't know *what* I'm saying, but out of fairness to you, I'm going to try. Everything's been incredible, but for some reason, that's making me paranoid. I have to admit, paranoia has been my constant state since I met you."

Charlie frowned. "Why?"

"Because you're perfect. I mean, not literally, but you check everything on the proverbial list. Smart. Funny. Handsome. Kind. But you're also secretive, and I don't get it. I've noticed you skirting around telling me about certain parts of your life, but I've been telling myself that you must have some reason. If you were anyone else, I don't think I'd make excuses for you. Maybe this will spook you, but I've never felt this connected to someone so quickly, and hell, it's spooking me."

After Eli's speech, Charlie was quiet, staring up at the ceiling. The urge to kiss that long neck again was strong, but Eli stayed still. He could tell Charlie was thinking.

After a minute, Charlie looked at him. "I have terrible handwriting."

Eli blinked. "Come again?"

"It's true. My mom jokes that I should have been a doctor, it's so bad. Give me a crayon, and I can do a decent impersonation of a kindergartener. Oh, and I had to call a cleaning service before having you over, because I'm messy as fuck. When I sneeze, my entire body is involved, and I single-handedly perpetuate the stereotype that white people can't handle spicy food. That Thai food I brought you the other day is as hot as I can go before I literally start crying."

Eli thought back. "That wasn't even spicy."

"Exactly."

"Why are you telling me all this?"

"Because I'm not perfect. Not even close. I have plenty of flaws, and the ones I shared right then are scratching the surface. Wait for our first argument. Remember how you called me stubborn when we met? You ain't seen nothin' yet, babe. I know I'm not doing a great job of selling myself right now, but if you're in the market for non-perfect, you've found it."

Eli laughed. "All right, I guess that's fair. So, this doesn't freak you out at all?"

Charlie shrugged. "Maybe a little, but I'm not in the habit of questioning a good thing. I'll admit, there was a part of me in the beginning that thought my attraction to you was all physical. I mean, look at you." Charlie whistled. "I could expound. Then, I thought it was because you refused to give me your number at first. I love a good challenge; it comes with the stubborn territory."

Eli bit his lip. "Do you still feel that way?"

"Not even a little." Charlie reached over and took Eli's hand, twining their fingers. "I think we have a lot in common and that we work well together. I also think it's too soon to say much more than that. I'm not asking you to be my boyfriend or anything, but this feels good, and I don't just mean the sex. I'm not one to cast doubts on a relationship because it's going too *well*. And I think our chemistry is definitely real. Don't you?"

Eli nodded. "Last night was probably the most domestic date of my life, and I still wanted you every bit as much as when you were pulling a kid out of a burning building. It went a long way toward proving to me that this is real."

"Good. Though I'm still not in any rush. Let's take this one step at a time, okay? When are you free next?"

"I work all day today, but I'm not in until the afternoon on Sunday."

"Great. Come over after work? Spend the night with me, and we'll get brunch the next morning. I hear gay culture is all about brunch these days."

Eli laughed. "How about you come over to my place? I'll introduce you to my cats and take a turn making you dinner. My go-to dish is gumbo, but considering what you said about spice, I think I'll try something else."

"Deal." Charlie leaned in for a kiss.

Eli met him halfway, keeping it brief but firm. "Thanks for listening to me. I've been chewing on that for a while now. It felt good to talk about it."

"It's my pleasure. Now, if it's all the same to you, I want to cuddle until my stomach absolutely insists I get out of bed, and then I want eggs."

"So demanding." Eli wrapped Charlie up in his arms, feeling more content than he had in a long, long time. As they lay together, Eli found himself saying a silent prayer that things really could be this easy.

CHAPTER 8

A week passed, and it seemed as though the arsonist was on hiatus. On one hand, Eli was grateful no more fires were being set, for obvious reasons. On the other, he sincerely hoped the guilty party wasn't going on another years-long break. He wanted the bastard caught, for good.

Things at work remained tense as everyone waited to see what would happen next. They dealt with other issues—mostly rescue services; a long day of rain had caused flooding and stranded some people in their cars—but nothing could distract Eli from the arsonist. Not even his adorable sort-of-boyfriend.

Although, Charlie was hands-down the highlight of almost every day. They were constantly either together or texting about when they could next be together. Eli's cats had started perking up at the sound of Charlie's footsteps approaching the kitchen door. Charlie spoiled the crap out of them with special treats and fancy toys, but on days when he wasn't lavishing them, they still purred like mad when he was around.

Eli was admittedly a little jealous, but mostly he was relieved. He'd been waiting to see their reaction to him before giving himself official permission to start falling in love. If Pistol had hissed at Charlie the way he'd done to Eli's last boyfriend—the one who'd ended up cheating on him—Eli might have reconsidered the relationship.

But no, when Charlie slept over, Pistol curled up by his side. One morning, when Eli had been forced to rise early, he'd snuck a photo of them sleeping together. It was now the lock screen on his phone. He smiled every time he checked it.

Eli had Thursday night off this week, so he invited Charlie over without thinking about it. It was automatic to him now: free time equaled a date with Charlie. It'd been some time since he'd had his bed to himself for more than one night in a row, and he liked it that way.

He also couldn't remember the last time he'd had so much sex. His thigh muscles were still aching from the night before, when Charlie had attacked Eli on his sofa mid-Netflix marathon. He'd had Eli ride him until they were both sweaty, sore, and *satisfied*. It was worth every twinge of discomfort today. If this kept up, Eli would be able to cut his workout schedule down to three times a week.

Anette seemed to be living vicariously through his romance. She asked him about Charlie every time they saw each other. Eli enjoyed getting to talk about boys after his dating hiatus, but it highlighted a problem he was increasingly unable to ignore. The one dark cloud hanging over the relationship: Charlie's secret.

"You *still* don't know what he does?" The incredulity in Anette's voice was impossible to miss. She was leaning next to Eli's locker, watching him put away the last of his gear. His shift had ended, but hers was just beginning. "I thought you were worried it was something illegal."

"I was, and I still am. It bothers me every damn day." He closed his locker only to drop his head against it. The cool metal chilled his brow. "Anette, what am I going to do?"

"I dunno." She lowered her voice. "You still reckon he's dealing?"

"He's gotta be doing *something*, or he wouldn't keep dodging me. But it's so hard to believe the sweet, caring guy I know is mixed up in something like that. Maybe it's not illegal, and it's just . . . I don't know, bad? What if he works for a big, evil corporation?"

Anette shrugged. "Whatever he does, you need to stop playing and find out before you fall for this boy and set yourself up for some serious heartache."

She was right. The problem was, it was already too late for that. Charlie was a part of his life now, and if Eli had to say goodbye, it was going to break his heart.

Please, God, let this all work out.

Thursday evening found him in his kitchen, humming to himself as he stirred white wine into the salt, pepper, and butter mixture that was going to top some steamed shrimp. Right at seven o'clock, the kitchen door opened. A smile automatically spread over Eli's face. He loved that Charlie had stopped bothering to knock.

"Honey, I'm home!" Charlie elbowed his way in, a baguette and a bottle of wine tucked into the crook of his arm.

"Darling," Eli cooed back, turning away from the stove. "I told you not to bring anything."

"I know, *muffin*." Charlie stopped to set his wares on the counter before sidling up to Eli. "I hate to show up empty-handed, though."

They'd been toying with pet names lately. Their general consensus was that everything sounded ridiculous, so they'd made a game of it. As the night went on, they'd call each other increasingly ridiculous monikers. Whoever laughed first lost and had to make breakfast. Eli made breakfast a *lot*.

"Well, thank you." Eli kissed him. "That's very sweet."

Right on cue, the cats came bursting into the room, yowling up a storm. They swarmed Charlie's legs.

He laughed and bent down to give each of them a pat on the head. "I'm sorry, y'all. I don't have any presents this time. I'll make it up to you, I promise."

The cats brushed up against his legs a few more times, but when he failed to produce a treat, they lost interest. Well, Moxie and Chutzpah did. Pistol plopped down at Charlie's shoes, as usual. He was starting to feel more like Charlie's cat than Eli's.

Ignoring Pistol for now, Charlie slid his hands around Eli's waist, pulling him close. "I'm so glad to be here. I missed you. And honestly, after the day I had, I could use a home-cooked meal."

"Oh?" Eli moved to kiss him again but kept it light so Charlie could talk. "What happened? Was it work?"

Charlie tensed for a fraction of a second before pulling away. "Uh, no. It was a long day in general. Chores, errands, that sort of thing."

Normally, Eli would let it go, but he knew Charlie had gone to the "office" that day, because he'd set an early alarm the night before. "If it's work shit, you can vent to me. I still don't know anything about what you do." He held his breath as he waited for Charlie's response.

Charlie looked away. "Really, it's nothing. Tell me about your day."

Irritation swelled up in Eli's chest before he could check it. Seriously, hadn't this avoidance game gone on long enough? He pursed his lips, thinking. This was usually the point where he'd choose to ignore Charlie's evasiveness, take the out, and move on to more pleasant subjects. But after his talk with Anette, he didn't feel like doing that. He felt like getting some answers.

"My day was spent wondering why you still refuse to tell me where you spend forty hours a week."

Charlie's eyes widened. For a moment, Eli dared to hope he was going to crack. But then his features smoothed.

"You know where I was. I spent the day in the office, same as usual. I had to do a lot of paperwork, and of course my boss wants it all done yesterday. Now, I'm looking forward to relaxing with you. And I brought my appetite. What are you making?"

There was a part of Eli that honestly wanted to drop it. He had a pleasant evening of good food and great sex ahead of him. But each time Charlie dodged him, Eli got more and more annoyed. Did he think Eli was buying this whole charade?

"That won't work." Eli crossed his arms over his chest. "You can't change the subject and expect me to keep letting it slide. I told you last week there's clearly some reason why you're refusing to tell me, and you even dodged *that*. Don't think I didn't notice. This is important, Charlie. Why do you keep lying to me?"

"I'm not lying." Charlie's mouth opened and closed several times. "I don't want to fight."

"Great. Me neither. What do you do for a living?"

There was a long pause.

"I work in an office, and it really is a boring job that requires lots of paperwork nine days out of ten. Beyond that, I can't tell you. Not yet."

Eli laughed humorlessly. "Why not? You a spy or something?"

"I really can't say anything more right now."

Eli let out a frustrated breath. He reached for the dial on the stove and turned it all the way down to low. He had a feeling this was going to be a long conversation. "Seriously, babe, fess up. I can't take much more of this mysterious act. I don't know if this is meant to intrigue me, or what, but I'm done playing."

Charlie's mouth was agape. "You think I'm doing this for *attention*?"

"I didn't say that." Though he'd certainly implied it. "I can't think of why else you'd bait me like this. The only other explanations I can come up with are that your job is either repugnant or illegal. Potentially both. Do you sell drugs? Are you in a cult? What?"

"I'm not baiting you. This isn't about you at all. I said I can't tell you, and I meant it." Now Charlie sounded irritated. "I'm not trying to lie to you. I can't believe you think I'd do that."

"What else am I supposed to think? This is bizarre. My own boyfriend won't tell me what he does."

Silence doused the room like sudden rain. They'd talked about being boyfriends before, but neither of them had actually used the word.

Wow, my timing is fucking impeccable.

After an awkward beat, Charlie wet his lips. "Eli, I *hate* not telling you the whole truth, but I don't want to lie to you either. I could have made up some bullshit, but I didn't. Doesn't that count for anything?"

That gave Eli pause. For about five seconds. "I don't know. This is all a little too weird for me."

"What's that supposed to mean?"

Eli wasn't sure himself. He fell silent as he thought it over. If he was being honest, he'd have to admit that part of his irritation was aimed at himself. Charlie wasn't the only one keeping a secret. Eli had never told him he'd suspected Charlie of being the arsonist long after Charlie had directly said he wasn't.

Now, they were nearly a month into their relationship, and the window to have that conversation without it causing some serious shit was closing. But Eli kept dragging his feet, mostly out of fear of how Charlie would react. He hadn't trusted Charlie in the beginning, so what right did he have to ask for trust in return?

Then again, Eli was falling in love with him, more and more each day. Every time Charlie dodged a question about his past, Eli had to wonder exactly who he was falling in love with. His heart was on the line, and it wasn't fair for Charlie to make him take that gamble.

This all came down to the same questions Eli had been struggling to answer from the start: Did he trust Charlie? Did he believe Charlie had a good reason for not telling him? Did he believe Charlie would tell him the truth when he could? And if so, did Eli believe that what Charlie revealed wouldn't scare him away?

Eli ended up answering Charlie's question and his own at the same time.

"I have to do some thinking, Charlie." Eli turned away. He didn't think he could look Charlie in the eye right now. "If you can't be honest with me, then I have to decide if I'm all right with that or not. I've been under a lot of pressure at work, what with the arsonist and all. Maybe we should take a break until things are clearer."

His chest tightened with every word as if someone were screwing bolts into his ribs. Misery spiderwebbed through him. What really hurt, however, was the utter betrayal in Charlie's voice when he spoke next.

"You want to break up? Over this?"

"I'm not saying break up. I'm saying spend some time apart. It'll give us both a chance to figure out what we want." Eli moved to the sink, needing to put some distance between them. "How about this: when you can tell me the truth—all of it—then give me a call. Until then, I don't want to see you anymore."

"Eli, that's not—"

There was an unholy screech. Eli's head snapped over in time to see Pistol shoot out of the kitchen, nothing more than a vague black streak.

"Shit, I stepped on his tail." Charlie started forward like he intended to go after the cat, but he stopped by Eli's side. "Don't do this. What does it matter what I do for a living? We're happy, Eli. *Really* happy. I know you feel it too."

Eli shook his head. "I can't be happy with someone who isn't being totally honest with me."

Hypocrite.

There was a pause. He prayed Charlie was going to go quietly, but of course, he huffed angrily next to him.

"You're so full of shit."

Eli looked over, mouth open to deliver an irritable retort, but the sheer devastation on Charlie's face stopped him cold.

Charlie was actually shaking, and his eyes shone with unexpected brightness. "You've been looking for a reason to run from the start."

"I have not. I—"

Charlie held up a hand. "Don't accuse me of lying and then lie to my face. From the very beginning, you've pushed me away. I had to beg you to give me your number when we first met. Then you attributed the feelings between us to adrenaline and not our obvious connection. And *then* you asked if this was going *too well*. Now, you're pushing me away again."

Eli didn't have a good comeback. At least, not one that didn't involve telling Charlie he'd been distant because he'd suspected Charlie was a criminal to varying degrees. He kept his mouth shut.

Charlie continued. "You know what, Eli? You're right. I've kept things from you. But I've done it because every step of the way, you've seemed like you were looking for an out. I thought if I said one wrong thing, you'd spook. Turns out, that wasn't the case. I didn't even need to say anything."

Before Eli could protest, Charlie whirled around and stomped out of the kitchen the way he'd come in. Over his shoulder he shouted, "Apologize to Pistol for me, please. And the others. I'm going to miss them."

Unsaid words rang in Eli's ears.

And you.

After Charlie had left, Eli spent a long time staring at the door, replaying their conversation and wishing, despite everything, that he'd walk back in. It felt like Charlie had taken a part of Eli with him. One of his lungs, judging by how hard it was to breathe.

He knew his reasons for keeping Charlie at arm's length, and he stood by his assertion that he needed to know the truth before this went any further, but Charlie's accusations clung to him like stale smoke.

Anette had told Eli he was a self-saboteur. Was it possible that no matter what Charlie had done, Eli still would have gone looking for flaws? He said he wanted marriage and a family and a house one day, yet he always seemed to find some reason not to be with whoever he was dating. Was that because they weren't right for him, or was he finding faults wherever he could?

Was there some part of Eli that didn't think he deserved happiness?

Before he could delve too far into that frightening prospect, his phone rang. It was the siren ringtone he'd chosen for the chief. He snatched his phone off the kitchen counter.

"Hello?"

"Get down to the station right now, Johnson. There's been another fire."

Flames were still batting at the sky by the time Eli arrived at the abandoned warehouse downtown. Firefighters were running back and forth between the three trucks that'd been called to the scene, more than Eli had ever seen at one fire before.

EMS was standing by, as were the police. There wasn't a crowd yet, probably thanks to the isolated location. But no one would be able to miss the plumes of blacker-than-black smoke billowing into the sky for long.

Eli spotted Anette at the back of one of the trucks, readying oxygen for any victims of smoke inhalation. He jogged over to her. "What are our orders?"

"Eli." She turned around. Her raised voice was barely audible over the roar of flames and pounding water. "The chief is here somewhere, but I don't know where. Right now, we're working on containing the spread and making sure none of the other buildings go up."

He raised his voice to match hers. "Isn't this strange? The arsonist has always chosen public locations, and never this late at night."

"Maybe it's not him. We won't know until an investigation has been conducted. It could be a while."

"Do the search teams need an extra hand? Or the hoses?"

"The hoses are set, and no one's going into the building this time. It's too dangerous right now. Besides, it doesn't look like there was anyone inside. There were, however, some civilians in the area who have been detained for questioning. One of them could be the arsonist, for all we know. They're with the police, except for the guy getting some medical treatment."

Eli's heart started pounding. "Medical treatment?"

"Yeah, one of them tried to run into the building. Said he knew homeless people sometimes use these abandoned warehouses for shelter, and he wanted to check for victims. If he's telling the truth, the guy's a real hero."

The words ricocheted through Eli like a gunshot. He knew someone who resembled that remark. But it couldn't be. Could it? He'd just seen Charlie earlier that night. Then again, he'd left Eli's house more than an hour ago. That could have given him enough time to . . .

Please, God, don't let it be him. Not after all this.

"I'm going to check on the civilians." Eli's voice cracked, but thankfully it wasn't noticeable in the din. "Then I'll be back. If you see the chief, tell her I volunteer to go into the building and search for anyone who might be trapped."

She shook her head. "That's suicide, but you got it. I'll be here."

Eli gave her shoulder a reassuring squeeze before jogging off toward the line of EMS and police cars. Officers were setting up the usual barricades, though there was no crowd of reporters and bystanders yet to suppress. That made it easy for Eli to spot a group of out-of-place civilians. A handful were still getting checked out by paramedics, but the others were talking to an officer by her patrol vehicle. Giving statements, no doubt.

When his eyes landed unerringly on Charlie's dark head, a carousel of emotions spun through him: resignation, anger, regret, and a tiny twinge of surprise from the part of him that had believed, honest to God, that it couldn't be him.

That made three fires now. Charlie had been present at three of the four fires, and there was always a chance Eli had missed him at the previous one. Was there any way this could all be one giant coincidence?

The first fire had been the day they met. The second was their first date. And now this one? It was bringing them back together after their first fight. It was too much. The pattern was too clearly marked.

I was right. The words were tennis balls bouncing off the walls of Eli's skull. *I was right from the start. He's the arsonist. I should have trusted my gut. I should have stayed away from him. I never should have let myself fall. If people find out I dated the arsonist . . . what will happen to me?*

His mom's face flashed into his mind, as it always did in moments of crisis. If she were alive, what would she say? She'd probably think he was a damn fool.

As if on cue, Charlie glanced his way. Their eyes locked. For a second, neither of them moved, but then Charlie's expression darkened. He looked away. Perhaps he saw the betrayal that was certainly plastered on Eli's face, or he might still be angry about the fight earlier. Well, if he'd thought that was bad, it was nothing compared to what was coming.

Eli's first instinct was to go straight to Chief Sappenfield and tell her everything. His leg muscles were itching to turn him around and do precisely that, but he remained rooted to the spot. Cold realization washed over him like a tide.

If he told the chief the truth, he wouldn't be able to escape the consequences. He could already picture her disappointed face as she led him into her dreaded office to tell him what he already knew: he'd *really* fucked up.

It would've been one thing if Charlie and he had only gone on a couple of dates. He'd get reprimanded for that, of course, but he wouldn't be in any serious trouble. But now, he'd slept with Charlie. They'd been seen in public together, acting as a couple. Anette knew about them. So did Eli's dad.

When it came out that the boyfriend of a firefighter was the arsonist—and it would come out; these things always came out—it was going to be all over the news. Would he get run out of town like Billy Ray?

The chief wouldn't fire him. He was positive she'd be sympathetic toward him when he explained how he'd been duped. But with all the bad press sure to head their way, it wouldn't matter. Eli would resign rather than let his mistake tarnish everyone else. Chief Sappenfield. Anette. Rogers and McPherson. All of them.

What a perfect fool I've been.

The misery brewing in Eli's gut warped into anger. He'd known Charlie was lying to him, but this? This was another level. He didn't care what happened to him anymore. Charlie was going *down.*

As Eli was contemplating marching up to the nearest police officer and demanding they arrest Charlie, something occurred to him. When Eli had first suspected Charlie, he'd thought he had a hero complex. But if that was the case, why did he never want to talk to reporters? If he was doing this for attention or acclaim, why refuse to let anyone see him in action?

Eli couldn't fathom what his motive was. His head hurt from all this back and forth, like fucking whiplash. Nothing made any sense. For the sake of his aching heart, he should stop trying to mash the puzzle pieces together. He could hardly bear to think about it.

You know what you need to do. You want the truth? You have to give it first.

Fuck. Sometimes Eli hated the fair and rational parts of himself. Squaring his shoulders, he made a beeline for the group of civilians. Charlie watched him approach, expression unreadable.

When Eli got there, he greeted the officer and asked precisely what he'd ask under normal circumstances: Did any of the civilians see anything the FD needed to be aware of?

Officer Lopez immediately indicated Charlie, saying he'd run into the building. If anyone could give a helpful statement, it'd be him.

"Come with me," Eli said, voice flat. "I'd like to hear your statement firsthand, and then afterward, I'll hand you back over to the police. Or the paramedics, if you need additional medical attention."

Charlie went with him without complaint, for once. He seemed to hear in Eli's tone that there was no point in refusing.

The walk to the truck was silent. Eli focused on doing his job, what he should have been doing all along. When they arrived, everyone was too busy to notice them. Eli situated them out of hearing range anyway and then faced the fire.

They were beating it down, but it was slow going. The acrid smell of smoke stung his nostrils with every breath. It was going to take them hours to get the fire reduced enough for anyone to go inside. Until then, they wouldn't be able to investigate. And to think, Eli had the culprit next to him.

"So," Charlie said, tone a little too casual, "you getting déjà vu?"

Eli's head snapped toward him. "What?"

"This is almost exactly like when we met. I'd run into a burning building, you were taking my statement, and I was all covered in soot." He waved a hand. "Though there was a very different kind of tension between us, I suppose."

"This isn't funny, Charlie."

Charlie's brown eyes were somber. "I never said it was."

Eli considered putting on his mask, because working up the breath to say what he said next was a feat. "We need to talk."

This was the last kindness Eli could bestow on Charlie until he knew the truth. He was going to give Charlie a chance to explain himself. Eli would tell him everything, from the beginning, and see what Charlie had to say. For better or for worse, by daybreak tomorrow, everything would be out in the open.

"Right now?"

Eli shook his head. "Tonight. I don't know how long I'm going to be here, and I don't care. If I call you at one in the morning, you need to answer."

Charlie nodded. "Let me know when you get home, and I'll come over."

"No, I'll come to you." *If I have to call the police, it'll be easier to detain him in his own home.*

Just thinking that tied Eli's stomach into knots.

Charlie nodded again. "You know where my spare key is. If I'm asleep, let yourself in."

The thought of walking into Charlie's place and finding him asleep in bed, like he'd done a dozen times before after working a long shift, made Eli seriously worry he was going to throw up. He searched around for an escape.

McPherson happened to be jogging by. Eli grabbed him by the shoulder and whirled him around. "Can you escort this civilian back to Officer Lopez? The chief asked me to find her as soon as I got here." The lie was far too smooth on his tongue.

Something in Eli's tone must've sounded dire, because McPherson—never one to take orders from someone he had seniority over—nodded curtly.

Without another word, Eli walked away from Charlie and toward the fire. He didn't look back.

CHAPTER 9

Charlie sat at his kitchen table, fiddling with a half-eaten sandwich he'd lost interest in. He'd normally be exhausted at this time of night, but he'd never been less interested in sleep. Anticipation thrummed through him, making him antsy.

Despite the frostiness of their last encounter, he was looking forward to talking to Eli. This whole "break" thing was bullshit, and he intended to shove Eli's nose in it. If they spent time apart this early in the relationship, they'd both end up moving on. Pissed as Charlie was, he didn't want that to happen. Especially not over something so petty.

It was poetic in a morbid way that a fire had brought them together again. Charlie wasn't even supposed to be in that part of town, but thanks to a twist of fate, he'd ended up sprinting into yet another burning building. He'd intended to slip away before anyone saw him, like he'd been doing, but he was adult enough to admit he'd been hoping to catch a glimpse of Eli.

When they'd locked eyes, both bathed in the orange glow of the fire, Charlie's emotions hadn't known what to do. Anger as sharp and bright as the flames had mixed with the excitement and affection he felt whenever he saw Eli, leaving him rooted in place.

Charlie had expected Eli to do more of his avoidant fuckery, but instead he'd waltzed right over. Even more surprising, he was the one who'd proposed they talk. Charlie had been planning to give it a few days and then call him. So much for that. Judging by the determined look that'd been on Eli's face, he was done running.

Fine by me. Charlie sighed and pushed his plate away, suddenly unable to even look at food. *I'm so angry at him, and yet all I can think is that we have to make this work. Because the truth is, I'm so deeply, irrationally in love with Eli, I don't know what to do with myself. I know it's too soon, and I don't care. I can't let myself think this is the end.*

His phone buzzed. A quick glance confirmed what he suspected: a text from Eli.

You still awake?

Charlie typed the fastest reply of his life. *Yeah, I'm waiting on you.*

No chat bubble popped up to indicate Eli was responding. A second later, Charlie found out why. There was a knock on his door.

Frowning, Charlie got up from the table and made his way to the hall, the flooring cold beneath his bare feet.

When he opened it, Eli was standing outside in street clothes, hands shoved in his pockets and a grim set to his jaw.

Uh-oh. He looks ready for a fight.

"Should have told me you were on your way." Charlie looked down at himself. He'd changed out of his ashy clothes, but he'd waited to shower in case he couldn't hear his text notification. "I thought I'd have time to freshen up once I knew you were headed here."

Eli didn't respond. He stepped forward, indicating he was ready to come inside. Charlie moved back to make room for him, but for a second, they were sharing the doorway. That one instant was all it took to make a spark of attraction fly between them. Their eyes met, and Charlie briefly lost the ability to breathe.

The connection between us . . . I know he feels it too. This can't be for nothing.

"If it's all the same to you, I'd like to be sitting for this conversation." Eli moved past him toward the living room, and the moment shattered like glass.

Charlie followed him to the couch and sat a decent distance away from him. It was awkward, inserting this space between them on the same piece of furniture where they'd cuddled up a dozen times before. Judging by the tension in Eli's shoulders, however, this wasn't going to be fixed with a frantic make-out session.

"We need to talk." Eli looked at the ground.

"Yeah, we do." Charlie twisted in his seat so he was facing him. "You seem like you've got something to say, so if you want to go first, be my guest."

Eli glanced at him, and Charlie didn't think he'd ever seen his eyes look so flat. "I want to give you the chance to be honest with me. Right now. If you tell the truth, it'll be easier on you in the long run."

Charlie wasn't certain he understood that last bit, but he nodded. "You're right. I do need to be honest, and I have every intention of telling you everything. But first, I have to say how happy I am that you wanted to talk. I said earlier that you tend to run away, but here you are, and I think that means you want to work on this as much as I do."

Eli blinked at him. "What?"

"I said I think we should—"

"No, I heard you. Why are you talking about our earlier fight?"

It was Charlie's turn to blink. "Um, because that's why we're here? You wanted to talk about us? I know we both said some hurtful things, but—"

Eli cut him off again with a wave of his hand. "Who cares about the damn fight? Charlie, this is serious. If you did what I think you did, you could go to prison for a long time."

Okay, now Charlie was really lost. "Um, come again?"

Eli leaned toward him, eyes intense. "If you're honest with me, I can help you. No one got hurt, so if you turn yourself in, I think they'll go easy on you."

"What? Eli, I have no clue what you're saying right now."

"Don't lie to me, Charlie." Eli's voice rose. "Am I supposed to believe it was a coincidence that you were at the scene of almost every fire? Or that the fires all correlated to events in our relationship? I tried not to believe it, especially after talking to you about it, but setting these fires is obviously some way for you to get attention. You need help, Charlie."

Understanding washed over Charlie like ice water. Before he realized what he was doing, he jumped to his feet. "You . . . you still think I'm the *arsonist*?"

"I didn't for a long time, trust me. I believed you when you told me you weren't, and even Anette said there was no way. I kept telling myself, what are the chances? But after seeing you at tonight's fire, it was too much of a coincidence. If you tell me the truth, I promise I'll do everything I can to help you. I noticed before that the fires never seemed like they were meant to hurt anyone. I can testify to that fact."

Charlie had the most bizarre and inappropriate urge to laugh. It bubbled up in him, and right as he thought it would burst out, it changed into words. "I'm not the fucking arsonist, Eli. I'm an undercover cop!"

Silence descended on the room. Eli was staring at him, his expression caught somewhere between shock and disbelief. Charlie stared back for a moment before fumbling for an old cigar box he kept on his coffee table. He flipped open the lid and pulled out his badge, tossing it to Eli.

Eli caught it without taking his eyes off Charlie's face. Then, he slowly looked down. Gripping the badge hard, he stared at it like he couldn't believe it was really there.

Charlie broke the silence. "My name is Detective Charles Thorpe. I've been working on this case as Charlie Kinnear. I was a rookie detective three years ago when the fires began. They were my first big assignment. I asked to lead the reopened investigation when it became clear the arsonist had returned."

Eli stared at him blankly for five whole seconds before a gleam of understanding sparked in his eyes. "Charles Thorpe. The chief mentioned our department was cooperating with a Detective Thorpe. That's . . . that's *you*?"

"In the flesh." Charlie sat down heavily. "I have a reputation for being able to blend into a crowd. It makes me ideal for undercover operations. If I hadn't insisted on talking to you at that first fire, you never would have noticed me."

"That's definitely not true." Eli cleared his throat, ducking his head. "But why? Why go undercover at all?"

"Little-known fact: cops hate talking to the press. Before, when I was a rookie, the older detectives always stuck me with making statements whenever there was no way around it. My name was plastered all over the local news. There was always a chance someone might recognize it. People are much more willing to open up if they don't know they're talking to a cop. It was a good thing my photo never made it into any newspapers, or I wouldn't have been able to take this assignment."

Judging by the odd gurgling noise he made, Eli was attempting to piece this together. "So you . . . You really . . ." He took a breath. "I'm sorry. I have *so* many questions."

"Go ahead. I would too if I were in your shoes."

Eli shook his head. "Wasn't there a chance someone at the scene would recognize you anyway?"

"You tell me. When you're suited up, do people see you or your uniform?"

Eli answered without hesitation. "My uniform. We're all faceless proverbial firefighters to them."

"Exactly. When I worked this case before, I was a badge. Now, in plainclothes, I've had whole conversations with people who didn't recognize me without the uniform. It actually starts to fuck with your head after a while." Charlie didn't say the next sentence that formed on his tongue. *It was part of the reason why I wanted you to see me so badly.* "But I was careful to keep out of sight whenever possible. You saw how good I am at slipping away."

Eli scratched his chin thoughtfully. "If you're a cop, then why'd you act so dicey around them? Whenever they showed up, you headed straight for the nearest exit."

At that, Charlie had to laugh. "Because none of the beat cops in my precinct are Oscar-worthy actors. They spend their time writing speeding tickets and patrolling residential neighborhoods. It wouldn't surprise me if one of them slipped up and called me Thorpe in public. I didn't want to risk interacting with them in front of anyone."

Eli was quiet for a moment. "Why'd you hit on me? Wouldn't that blow your whole operation?"

Charlie looked at him askance. "Not if I didn't tell you the truth until after we'd caught the arsonist, which was my plan."

"I guess." Eli stared down at his hands. "Why risk it, though?"

That was actually a move Charlie had agonized about more than once, though he would never tell Eli that. At the time, it'd been an impulse. He'd seen a cute guy, and he'd gone for him. Five seconds after answering Chief Bakay's page, Charlie had been convinced he'd blown the whole operation. Eventually, he'd calmed down and had decided to give balancing a boyfriend and a secret identity a try.

Charlie chewed on his lip before answering. "You know why, Eli. Because I like you. I think using a fake name made me bold too, like wearing a mask at a ball."

"You mentioned that you don't normally do the pursuing."

"That's true. And I didn't expect us to get serious so quickly. I thought the case would be over before we had a chance to do more than go on a few dates, and then I'd be able to tell you everything. But we connected easily, and it wasn't like I could give up on the case. I took it hard when the arsonist disappeared before, like I'd failed my first big mission. This was supposed to be my second chance. Obviously, it didn't go according to plan."

"But *how* did you manage to be at the scene of so many of the fires? Before first responders even?"

"This information was never released to the public, but someone calls in an anonymous tip before every fire. We think it's the arsonist himself telling us ahead of time where he's going to strike."

"Why not evacuate wherever the tip is, then?"

Charlie smiled bitterly. "If only life were that easy. We didn't evacuate the school because we had no reason to think the serial arsonist was back. He technically wasn't yet, and we get a lot of tips. I mean, a *lot*. Mostly nonsense: kids calling in pranks and people spying on their neighbors. It gets worse when a criminal is at large. If we listened to every tip, we'd evacuate half the city. Instead, a few plainclothes officers scope out the promising ones. I usually go with my gut, and as you've seen, my gut is pretty damn accurate."

"What about our lunch date? You invited me to a place where you suspected there was going to be a fire?"

Charlie shook his head. "The deli was a coincidence, I swear. I was out of the office when that tip was called in, so that was a case of wrong-place, wrong-time."

"Wow." Eli blew out a breath. "This is a lot to process."

"Yet another reason why I wanted to do a gentle reveal." Charlie sat back in his chair. "Take all the time you need."

But it seemed Eli wasn't quite finished asking questions yet. "So, who do you think the arsonist is? You must have suspects."

"Nothing concrete, really. The theory is that the arsonist either wants to get caught or wants the attention for some reason."

"Damn. That's exactly what I told Chief Sappenfield. I knew the fires were never the point." Eli scrubbed a hand down his face. "I can't believe it. You were a cop the whole time. It all makes sense now."

"Yeah." Charlie smiled. "Now you know the truth."

Eli nodded. "Finally. I guess it all worked out in the end."

There was a pregnant pause.

The next second, they were both jumping to their feet.

"Wait a minute," they said simultaneously.

"You still lied to me about *everything*," Eli said. "Even your own name."

"You thought I was the arsonist after I explicitly told you I wasn't. You *slept* with me while you suspected I was a criminal."

They both fell silent, and the quiet was deafening in the wake of all that had been said. They stared at each other, barely breathing. Charlie had an odd moment of clarity in which he realized Eli and he were both thinking the same thing: there was a level of mistrust here that tapped into serious, ugly emotions. Deception. Resentment. Anger. While they'd been living in their blissful little bubble of secrets, they'd been laying down the groundwork for their own misery.

"Okay." Eli took a half step back. "Guess we gotta unpack this a little at a time. Why didn't you just tell me the truth from the start? I'm a firefighter. I serve the public same as you. Did you think you couldn't trust me to keep quiet?"

"It's not that. When you're undercover, you can't go around telling every cool new person you meet. We've only been dating for a month." He made a helpless gesture. "And honestly, I wasn't sure how you'd react. I dunno if you've turned on the news lately, but cops and the black community have issues, to put it far too lightly."

Eli shook his head. "I work with the police department all the time."

"I get that, but do you remember my friend Amos that I mentioned? I asked him about it, and he said I needed to give you a chance to see me as more than a badge first."

"I guess that's fair. I still think you should have trusted me."

"Like how you trusted me all those times you thought I was the arsonist? Didn't continuing to date me seem like a giant conflict of interest to you?"

"Of course it did. When I came in here tonight planning to confront you, I thought I was going to lose my job." Eli hesitated. "But honestly, before I saw you at tonight's fire, I'd genuinely convinced myself you weren't the arsonist after all. I thought—" He clamped his mouth shut.

Charlie eyed him. "You thought what?"

Eli looked sheepish. "Uh, remember that joke I made about how only doctors and drug dealers have pagers these days?"

Charlie stared blankly at him for a moment before realization hit him over the head. "Oh my God, you thought I was a *drug dealer*?"

"Kind of, yeah. But a little one. Like a dude who sells weed to his friends or something."

"Oh, well, that makes it all better." Sarcasm dripped from Charlie's tongue. "Arsonist or drug dealer. You sure had a hell of an impression of me."

Eli fixed him with a bland look. "It was just a theory. I had other ones too, some of which I told you when we argued."

"It doesn't matter. As a cop, having someone think you're a criminal isn't a fucking joke. What would you have done if I'd been dealing? Would you have left me? Were you dating me this whole time knowing it could end any second?"

Eli's complete silence was better than an answer.

That was just about Charlie's bullshit limit. "Why did you come here tonight? Why not turn me in?"

"I wasn't a hundred percent sure, and I wanted answers. Mostly, I wanted to know why a sweet, funny guy like you would do something like that. I asked myself what my mom would do in this situation, and here I am."

"Your mom would have given me a chance to come clean?"

"No, she would have hauled you down to the police station by the ear. I made the decision to hear you out. I've realized some things since I've met you. One of them is that my mom, great as she was, had a black-and-white view of the world, pardon my phrasing. Good. Bad. Hero. Criminal. You've made me want to take a closer look at the gray."

That was a hell of a statement coming from Eli, but it wasn't enough to assuage Charlie's anger. All this time, Eli had doubted him.

The one thing that Charlie had been completely honest with him about, Eli had disregarded the instant things got rocky. Eli, who was supposed to know him. Care about him. Maybe even love him some day.

Charlie had made his fair share of mistakes too, and if he were a bigger person, he might apologize. But this was all too much. Eli had come here tonight to take him to jail. In a crystalline moment of clarity, it hit him that he wasn't sure he could forgive that.

He needed time to think.

"Get out."

The words left his throat before he'd noticed his brain was forming them.

Eli hesitated before offering him a small smile. "I love that movie."

Charlie didn't so much as twitch. "I'm serious, Eli. I want you to leave."

"Okay." Eli stepped away like he intended to go, but then he turned around again. "Shouldn't we talk about this first? Don't get me wrong, I'm mad as hell, and I'm going to need a rundown of everything you told me about yourself that wasn't true, but I don't want to leave things like this."

With a shaky hand, Charlie rubbed his eyes, mortified to discover he was close to tears. "A mall. A hospital. A fucking elementary school. There was a part of you that thought, even for a second, that I was capable of starting fires in places that had *children* in them. Sick people and kids, Eli. I know it's only been a month, and I looked suspicious as hell for a minute there, but I don't know if I can be with someone who thought I was capable of that."

Eli was silent for a long spell. "I prayed it wasn't true. I actually clasped my hands together like I did when I was a kid and prayed to God. I dated you because I was convinced you couldn't have done that. You convinced me every day. You were so . . . good. Tonight, when I saw you at the fire, I was angry at you for keeping things from me, and I lost sight of that."

Charlie had heard enough. "I need time to process. You can let yourself out."

Eli didn't argue with him. Charlie kept his eyes down, but he heard the sound of Eli's feet retreating, followed by the soft *whoosh* of the front door opening and then clicking shut.

Charlie couldn't say how long he stood in his living room, fighting back tears, but eventually, one small sob wrenched its way out of him. It echoed pathetically in the empty apartment. He forced himself to raise his head, blinking back tears all the while. His living room looked strange to him. Too bright and far too big for one person.

In the kitchen, he poured himself a glass of water and forced it down his throbbing throat. He replayed his entire relationship with Eli from the start, only now, in the context of Eli thinking he was some form of criminal or another, everything was different. Darker. Shaded by lies and misconceptions.

As fresh anger sparked up within him, so did other emotions, namely regret and yearning. He should have told Eli the truth as soon as they'd gotten serious. He'd fucked up, and he accepted that. But he also understood why he'd done it. What he couldn't get a grasp on was what the hell he was going to do now.

With a sigh, he pulled his phone out of his pocket, already knowing who he needed to talk to. It was late as hell, and she was going to be pissed, but this was an emergency.

Charlie found his sister's name in his contacts and hit the Call button. It rang four full times, and just as Charlie feared he was going to get her voice mail, the line clicked.

"Your house had better be on fire." Kathryn's sleep-thick voice suggested what Charlie had feared: he'd woken her.

"Funny you should mention fire. Sorry to call so late, sis, but I need some advice."

"If this is about work, then for the hundredth time, tell that asshole from the sixth precinct to take his forty years of latent homophobia and shove them right up his—"

"It's not that, Kat. It's my love life."

There was a sharp intake of breath. "You have a love life again?"

"Had, more like it. I met this guy, and—"

Charlie's story was interrupted by a distant but ear-splitting wail. Kathryn sighed, and then came a sound that smacked of someone being hit repeatedly with a pillow.

"Mason," Kathryn said. "Mason, wake up. It's the baby."

A muffled man's voice said, "It's your turn to change her."

"I'm on the phone with Charlie. It's an emergency."

There was a prolonged, pained groan. "All right, but only 'cause you grew the kid 'n' all." Mason yawned and then must've leaned in toward the phone, because his next words were clear as day. "Hi, Charlie!"

"Hi, Mason!" Charlie called back.

After a pause, a much-more-awake-sounding Kathryn said, "Tell me everything."

Conscious of the late hour, Charlie gave her a thorough but quick recap of everything that'd happened in the past few weeks, from the serial arsonist's return to his relationship with Eli. Describing the fight was almost as bad as living through it, especially when Kathryn clucked her tongue like Mom did when she disapproved of something.

"Congrats, Charlie," she said. "You've made a hell of a mess."

"Hey, I had help. It's not like Eli is blameless in this."

"Ever hear the phrase 'two wrongs don't make a right'?"

Charlie sighed. "Yeah, I know. I'm angry in a way I can only imagine the ouroboros feels when it reaches its own neck. What should I do?"

"Honestly, lil bro, I'm not sure. What do you want to do?"

"Go back in time and change everything."

Kathryn hummed. "By 'change,' do you mean never meet Eli, or fix your mistake?"

Charlie knew the answer instantly. "I don't regret meeting Eli. I'm angry at him, but I wouldn't take back the time we had together."

"I think that's what you need to keep in mind, even if you two don't work things out. You can still learn something from all this, like how it's not cool to keep secrets from your boyfriends."

"I *really* didn't have a choice." Charlie sat down heavily on his sofa. "Seriously, 'undercover' isn't a word I use for fun. But I get what you mean. I should have kept things casual with Eli until I was in a place where I could tell him the truth. I just . . ."

Kathryn was silent, but when he failed to finish his sentence, she prompted him. "You what?"

"You know how I'm always saying I want to take things slow and do it right when it comes to relationships? With Eli, it was the opposite. We couldn't seem to move fast enough. Everything fell into place like it was meant to be. I felt like you for once. I knew what I wanted, and I went for it. So, why didn't I get my perfect happy ending?"

As if in response, another shriek sounded over the speakers. Charlie could picture Kathryn sitting up in bed and shouting into the adjacent nursery. "Hun? Everything okay?"

"I got this!" was Mason's distant reply.

"Charlie, let me assure you of one thing: I may have gotten everything I wanted, but that doesn't mean my life is perfect. Sometimes, even when things work out, they don't go the way you intended. Now, I wouldn't trade a single sleepless night, but that doesn't mean I'm not cranky as all hell in the morning. You get what I'm saying?"

"Sort of, I think."

"I'll be blunt, because I need to sleep: just because things between you and Eli aren't perfect doesn't mean they aren't right. I've seen you flake out on dozens of guys before and choose your work over love again and again. If this guy broke your pattern, he must be something special."

"How can you be so sure? You don't know him."

"No, but I know *you*. I know why you always want to take things slow: because you're stubborn, and once you make the decision to pursue something, you never stop. You wouldn't have given your heart to this guy if some part of you hadn't known it was safe with him. I'm not saying instantly forgive him—because I do think he fucked up and kept things from you as well—but you should think about how you hurt him too, and what you really want."

That seemingly innocuous advice shook Charlie like a branch in a storm. What the hell *did* he want?

"Thanks, sis. You've given me a lot to consider. I'll let you get back to bed."

"All right." She yawned. "Let me know what happens. Love you."

"Love you too."

He ended the call and slumped in his seat. The question Kathryn had raised wasn't going to be an easy one to answer. A month ago, it would have been: he wanted to catch the bastard who'd eluded him three years ago. On some level, he knew it wasn't his fault the arsonist had disappeared, but that hadn't stopped him from blaming himself.

He'd been too new to the force back then. Too green. He had to have missed something: a clue or a crucial piece of evidence. He'd thought he'd botched his first real chance to prove himself to all the other older detectives. After the arsonist had disappeared, he'd thrown himself into work, always trying to make up for the mystery he'd failed to solve.

When the fires had started up again, he'd been determined to close this case once and for all. He'd begged Chief Bakay to make him the lead investigator, and going undercover had seemed like their best chance to finally catch this motherfucker in the act. Charlie was great at blending in. Always had been. Although the second he'd met Eli, being invisible hadn't sounded so appealing anymore.

Why had he wanted so badly for Eli to see him? To the point where he'd risked the investigation, his own supposed redemption? What had changed?

You know what. You fell in love. At some point, the case stopped being the most important thing to you, only you were too stubborn to see it. You chose it over Eli, and that's the real reason you're in this mess.

Charlie might not have all the answers, but now he knew a few things for sure: Eli had made him feel like it didn't matter what his parents thought, or if he fucked up at work. He'd made Charlie feel like a hero. No one had ever done that for him before. Maybe no one ever would again.

There was another question he needed to answer. When he caught the arsonist, would it be as fulfilling as he'd always imagined? Or at the end of the day, was he still going to have this hole in his chest? The one that he swore had started to fill the moment he'd laid eyes on Eli?

"What am I supposed to do?" he whispered to himself.

If he were at Eli's house right now, he could count upon a meow of response, usually from Pistol. It pained him to think he might never see his adopted furry children ever again. Almost as much as the thought of never seeing Eli again.

His attention slipped to the case, the thing that'd started this domino effect. He'd thought "*when* he solved it" a second ago, but in truth, as of tonight, that'd become an "if." Last time, the arsonist had disappeared after four fires. If forensics indicated that tonight's incident at the warehouse had been caused by him, then he might very well disappear again, like last time.

The old Charlie would have thrown everything he had into catching him while he still could. But somehow, the idea of doing that now seemed so . . . hollow. As empty as his apartment. As his life.

Thoughts churning, Charlie heaved himself up and slunk off to his equally empty bed.

CHAPTER 10

"The fire at the warehouse was *not* the work of the arsonist."

Eli let out a tight breath at the same time as the dozen other firefighters around him.

Chief Sappenfield was standing in front of Dottie III, and they'd all gathered around her like schoolchildren waiting to hear a story. Her expression was as sharp as ever, despite the dark circles under her eyes. Eli had seen her resting on the cots upstairs more than once this week. When was the last time she'd gone home?

She cleared her throat to quiet them. "The arson investigator's report stated that faulty wiring had caused the fire. It makes sense. This fire didn't follow the arsonist's pattern. It happened late at night, in an isolated area, and it actually did some damage. There's good news and bad news. Bad news: the arsonist is still out there. Good news: The arsonist is still out there. If he follows the four-fire MO from last time, he will strike again. But that means we might have another chance to catch this bastard."

The people around Eli whooped. He remained silent, anxiety rending his guts into ribbons. The chief went on to hand out assignments and discuss schedule changes, all of which flew over Eli's head. His thoughts buzzed between the arsonist, Charlie, and all the questions that'd been answered last night.

He'd barely slept, instead choosing to spend his evening replaying the fight over and over again, like a recurring nightmare. The agony on Charlie's face when he'd told Eli to go was a particular highlight. He'd looked so torn, as if he'd hated ordering Eli away, but he'd done it anyway. He must've been furious.

With good reason. You accused the lead investigator on this case of being the serial arsonist. Nice one.

Pissed as Eli still was about being lied to, he could see Charlie's side of things with perfect clarity. Or *Charles's* side. Did he go by Charlie, or was that part of his undercover identity? Fresh anger surged through him at the thought. Part of him wanted to call Charlie and demand answers, but another, much more insistent part couldn't handle the thought of talking to him right now. Not while he was still so confused.

"Johnson. You okay?"

Eli's eyes had drifted to the cement floor, but at that, they nipped up. At some point, the others had left, leaving him standing alone in the center of the garage. How had he not noticed that?

Chief Sappenfield was eyeing him as if she were checking for signs of head trauma. "You got something on your mind?"

"I'm fine, Chief." Eli cleared his throat. "Maybe a little distracted. I'll get it together."

"No need. I want you to go home."

Eli's mouth fell open. "What? But, Chief, you said the arsonist is going to strike again. We need all the help we can get."

"I appreciate that, but you've been distracted all day, and considering the number of shifts you've been pulling lately, it's no wonder. You're burned out. I want you to rest."

"I can take a nap upstairs."

"No. You're no good to me like this. I need you sharp and focused. Go home. Eat something. Sleep in your own bed. When you've recharged, you can come back. Consider this an official order."

Eli's lips twitched. "There's no sense in arguing, is there?"

"Not unless you want a citation." Despite her harsh words, she gave his shoulder a light squeeze. "I know what you're feeling right now. The waiting around is the worst part. You feel helpless, so you want to control whatever you can. I get that—trust me—but you have to take care of yourself."

"You're one to talk, you know. When was the last time you went home?"

"Never you mind. I'm the battalion chief. That's my job. Besides, I'm not the one who's going to be out in the field keeping people safe."

"All right, I guess." He sighed. "I dunno how I'm ever going to sleep, though."

His expression must've flickered, because Chief Sappenfield frowned. "Is there something going on? No offense, but you don't look too hot. It's not your dad, is it?"

"No, he's fine. I had lunch with him last week." Eli paused, debating if he wanted to have this conversation with a superior. "I'd kill for some advice, but the matter is . . . personal."

"Gotcha. I won't pry. How about some general words of wisdom?"

"Lay it on me."

"One of the big downsides of this job is we sometimes see horrible things. Crimes, gruesome injuries, and deaths. But having that perspective gives us a chance to prioritize. When shit is hitting the fan in my personal life, I like to ask myself a question: Is what's going on as bad as a serial arsonist targeting hospitals and schools?"

That outlook caught Eli by surprise. In his head, his "huge" problems were suddenly cut down to size. When he thought about how many people those fires could have hurt, his fight with Charlie seemed like a blip. Still important to him, of course, but nothing in the grand scheme of things.

"Thanks, Chief. That actually helped."

"Don't sound so surprised." She smiled, all teeth. "Now get out of here before I write you up."

Eli scurried off. On the way out, he caught Anette's eye. She gave him a cheerful wave only to do a double take and furrow her brow.

Damn it, why did his emotions have to be so easy to read on his face?

Sure enough, before he'd so much as gotten in his car, his phone buzzed. He had a text from Anette.

What's wrong? You look mad as hell.

He considered telling a partial lie and claiming he was worried about work but decided against it. Anette had been right about Charlie not being the arsonist. Maybe she'd have some more valuable insight.

It's Charlie, he texted back before putting his phone away and starting his car. He'd planned on heading home, but his empty pantry flashed into his mind. After cooking for two these past few weeks, he needed to do some shopping.

He headed for his neighborhood grocery store. Right as he pulled into the parking lot and got out, Anette texted again.

What happened? Did you guys fight?

That made Eli laugh bitterly as he headed inside. What was the question version of an understatement? An underquestion?

The market wasn't busy, which made sense, considering it was the middle of the work day. Most of the people milling about were retirees or parents with small children. Eli slung a basket over his arm so he could text back.

Yeah, in a big way. We broke up.

The text had barely sent when Anette's contact photo popped up on his screen, along with an incoming call.

Sighing, Eli accepted it. "I'm shopping. Can we talk later?"

"Why do you ask questions you already know the answer to?"

"Fair enough." Eli headed for the produce section, his phone held between his shoulder and ear as he picked out a bag of spinach and a couple of crisp green apples. "You were right about Charlie not being the arsonist."

"I know that. I thought you knew it too."

Eli flinched. Hindsight being twenty-twenty, he now couldn't believe he'd turned on Charlie as quickly as he had. "About that. I sort of told Charlie my whole theory about him being a master criminal."

Anette sucked in an audible breath. "And he dumped you?"

"There's more to it than that, but yeah." After swearing Anette to secrecy, Eli filled her in, starting with the fight about Charlie's job and working up to the big reveal. By the time he'd finished, his basket was loaded. He headed for the shortest checkout line. "So after that, he told me to get out of his house, and I did. Now I have no idea what to do. Should I call him?"

"Are you still mad at him?"

"Of course I am. He lied to me in a big-ass way. He kept lying to me for weeks. But I also get why he did it, and let's be real: I fucked up too. Maybe not as bad as he did, but . . . Man, his face. Pure betrayal. I can't stop picturing it."

"He still lied, and that's not something you should forget simply because you also made mistakes."

"I think so too." It was Eli's turn in line. "Let me call you back after I check out."

"You'd better."

He pocketed his phone, paid, and walked out of the store with the bag cradled in one arm so he could hold his phone with the other.

"Welcome back," Anette chirped when she answered his call. "So, what are you going to do?"

"I was hoping for your advice on that, actually."

"Well, obviously you need to talk to Charlie. But I also think you need to deal with your issues as well. Why did you find it so hard to trust Charlie? Why were you so quick to think the worst of him?"

Eli reached his car and leaned against it. "I had good reasons for suspecting him, for one thing. But honestly, I think it's because he was so perfect for me. You know what they say about things that seem too good to be true. All my instincts were screaming at me that he was the one. I guess I got scared."

"Is that the whole reason?"

He sighed. "Also, I'm a self-saboteur who thinks I don't deserve good things, and you're always right, and Anette is the queen of the universe. Even Beyoncé bows before her."

"Damn straight. Identifying the problem is half the battle. Now you need to learn to let yourself be happy. And you need to get Charlie to talk to you, whatever it takes."

"Oh good. I thought you were going to suggest something difficult. If I have time leftover, maybe I'll invade Russia in the winter."

"Sounds like a plan. I have to get back to work. Call me later?"

"Sure thing. Oh, and Anette?"

"What?"

"Thank you."

She laughed. "You can thank me by inviting me to the wedding. I've been toying with the term 'groomsmaid.' Thoughts?"

"I love it. Talk to you soon." He ended the call, a smile on his face for the first time all day.

Right as he'd finished loading his groceries into the back seat, a flash of movement in his periphery caught his attention. Eli turned his head and spotted a figure in a black hooded jacket booking it across the parking lot.

"Someone must've realized he left his oven on," Eli muttered to himself. He was about to get into his car when a second figure appeared, in hot pursuit of the first. Eli did a double take. Even from this distance, there was no mistaking him.

Charlie.

Eli started forward before he'd realized he was moving. The two were running away from the street, toward a series of old buildings across from the grocery store. They were going to shoot right past Eli. The buildings had little alleys between them. He'd bet money one of them was the fleeing man's destination.

So many things happened so quickly, it rattled Eli's brain. First, a distant alarm split the air. Then, he spotted black smoke curling up from the back of the grocery store. And—most importantly of all—Charlie spotted him.

Eli was too far away to make out the details of Charlie's expression, but something like relief washed over his face.

"Eli!"

That was all Charlie said, but it was enough, somehow, to let Eli know precisely what he needed to do. Even so, for a split second, he vacillated. His first instinct—an instinct that had been drilled into him over the course of the past five years—was to run toward the fire. See if anyone was hurt. Get everyone out. Keep it from spreading. But the urgency in Charlie's voice was ringing in his ears, and he made a snap decision.

He sprinted after the hooded figure.

Eli tried to cut him off, but the guy saw him coming and swerved, keeping his face carefully turned away. His trajectory would send him straight into one of the alleys, and once there, he'd have a dozen buildings and side streets he could use to disappear. If they were going to catch him, they had to do it *now*.

Focused as Eli was on running after the criminal, he almost didn't notice when Charlie caught up with him. They were running side by side—Eli could just imagine their hearts pounding in unison—and even as raw determination flooded into him, something else did too.

Completeness. An utter and defining certainty that he was right where he was supposed to be. Next to Charlie.

That feeling lasted for all of three seconds before it was replaced with nerves as taut as bowstrings. The alleys loomed up before them, and though Eli was running as fast as his screaming lungs could bear, he wasn't gaining any ground. The fleeing figure was a handful of yards ahead of him, so close and yet so far. He'd been running for longer, but the power of flight-or-fight could keep him going for God knew how long.

Don't let him get away. He can't get away.

Eli had to do something. Had to give it everything he had and either succeed or fail. As a plan formed in his mind, he knew there was a good chance he was going to look back on this move for the rest of his life and see it as his biggest regret. But he also knew what he had to do.

Right at the mouth of the alleys, Eli poured everything he had into one final, soul-tapping burst of speed. The guy was fast, but for ten interminable seconds, Eli was faster. All those hours spent in the gym—working to be strong enough, quick enough—paid off in that one moment.

He full-body tackled the guy and sent them both flying onto the hot pavement. The sound that escaped from the criminal was like a deflating tire. Eli's skin burned where it scraped the ground, but the pain barely registered. All his focus was on his arms as they locked around the guy's neck and torso. If he tried to run, he was in for a hell of a fight.

As it turned out, there was no need. On his way down, the guy's face smacked the pavement, and he went limp. Eli maneuvered into a squatting position next to him, one hand fisted in his clothes in case it was an act.

Seconds later, Charlie skidded to a stop feet from them, kicking up plumes of cement dust. "Is he out?"

"I think so." Despite already knowing the answer, Eli asked, "The arsonist?"

"Yup. I caught him red-handed at the scene."

Charlie pulled out a pair of handcuffs, gathered the guy's arms behind his back, and slapped them on his wrists like he did this every day. Which, Eli realized, he very well might. His brain went to all sorts of inappropriate places.

Charlie let out a slow breath. "Jesus, my heart's still pounding."

"Mine too."

He looked at Eli askance. "I thought for sure you were going to run for the fire instead of stopping him."

"Honestly, I thought I was too for a second there, but some part of my brain screamed at me that if we didn't catch him now, we were going to lose him again. Maybe forever this time." He put on his presentation voice. "Prevention is an important aspect of fire safety."

Charlie laughed and then pressed his lips together, as if to stop himself. "Thank you. Do you need to go?"

Eli wanted so badly to know who the arsonist was, but it was true he should head for the store. Without proper gear, there wasn't much he could do, but he could help evacuate.

As he debated, another more familiar siren sounded, followed shortly by the appearance of Dottie III. The truck headed around the building, following the smoke. Judging by the tiny plume, it was probably another inconsequential dumpster fire.

Eli's radio hadn't gone off, so he hadn't been summoned to the scene. A stream of people spilled out of the building, more or less without panic. Everyone was doing what they were supposed to do.

"Talk fast." Eli pulled out his phone. "I'll text the chief while you fill me in."

"We got a bunch of anonymous tips today. The most promising one said the fire was going to be at a convenience store, but I wasn't so sure. My gut said it'd be here. I've been canvassing the place all morning. He got sloppy, like they always do when they've gotten away with it enough times." Charlie's grin was downright wicked, in the best way.

Eli had been struggling to catch his breath before, but now he suspected it was because Charlie was standing close to him, all triumphant and sweaty and flushed from exertion. Damn, he was sexy like this. "You sound like one of the gritty, loose-cannon cops on TV."

Charlie laughed, this time without reservation. He smiled at Eli, looking so much like the first time they met. When their eyes locked, something crackled between them.

"The second I saw you, I knew we had him." Charlie had stopped panting, and yet he still sounded breathless. "I actually thought to myself 'Eli's here. It's going to be all right.'"

Emotions swirled in Eli's chest, ranging from elation to confusion. "Charlie, I—"

Charlie grabbed his face and kissed him. Hard. Eli didn't hesitate for a second before kissing back. God, it felt good to touch Charlie. Like his lungs were back from vacation, and he could breathe normally again. Like everything made sense.

For a second, he reveled in it. But then the fight slammed back into Eli's mind, along with all the lies and confusion. The adrenaline drained out of him, leaving him feeling empty.

In a flash, they both seemed to realize what they were doing. They broke away, breathing hard. Charlie's lips were red, his eyes wild. He opened his mouth, but he never got the chance to speak. More sirens were coming to life all around them, converging on this spot. Any second now, the place would be crawling with first responders.

They exchanged knowing looks.

"Deal with this later?" Charlie asked.

Eli nodded, never taking his gaze from Charlie's face. "Later."

"Good. Let's see who our arsonist is." Charlie pulled the guy's hood back, revealing a white man, early thirties, with a clean-shaven, generically attractive face.

"Holy shit," they said in unison.

"The Channel 8 news guy?" Charlie's tone was incredulous. "The one who had that viral video about Billy Ray Phelan?"

"That's him all right." Eli frowned. "Why would he set a bunch of fires?"

Charlie shrugged. "Beats me. I'm just glad we caught the bastard. I can't read him his rights while he's unconscious. Guess that'll have to wait."

Eli nodded. "I'm going to see if everyone evacuated safely. Unless you want me to stay with you?"

Charlie blinked.

Eli waved a hand. "Not like that! I meant in case this guy wakes up and tries to escape."

"We made him, and he's cuffed. He's not going anywhere." Charlie pulled a black radio out of his pocket. "Let me call this in. Get some warrants going. I wasn't kidding when I told you this job involves a lot of paperwork."

Eli laughed, genuinely at first and then awkwardly as that statement settled in. "When EMS arrives, I'll send a paramedic over to make sure I didn't give him a concussion or anything. He hit his head pretty hard."

"Thanks." Charlie paused. "You did good work, Eli. I don't know if I could have chased him down without you."

"I'm sure you would have."

The sirens were cacophonic. Police, EMS, and Eli's crew swarmed the area. It was a miracle Chief Sappenfield hadn't called him yet.

He started to head off but then stopped. "Listen, Charlie, I think we should talk about last night. Sooner rather than later."

Charlie wouldn't quite meet his gaze. "I think so too. I don't want you to get the wrong idea, though. That kiss before . . . That was adrenaline. We're not okay."

"I get that. I don't expect it to be an easy conversation. I'll call you when all of this has quieted down?"

"Let me call you."

It was probably the best that Eli could have hoped for. "Okay."

As familiar sirens rang in his ears, he jogged toward the grocery store, heart pounding for more than one reason.

Charlie read through his report three times, checking every crossed *t* and dotted *i*. It was pages thick, much longer than what he usually typed up. As well it should be. This was no run-of-the-mill jaywalking case the chief would set his coffee on. This was Charlie's redemption.

He'd done it. He'd caught the guy. After three long years, the Louisville arsonist was behind bars. Hours later, it still hadn't fully hit him. It was over.

His computer hummed on the cluttered desk, begging him to close the twenty tabs he'd had open for the past week. The clock on the nearby wall ticked away. Charlie avoided looking at it so he wouldn't know how late it was.

He'd gotten out of the interrogation room and had come straight here to type everything up. The sooner they got this bastard processed, the better. Charlie's eyes wandered to a name in the report: Peter Lester, a local news anchor who'd let ambition get the best of him.

According to his confession, that was what this whole thing had been about. Ambition.

It was a wild tale from start to finish, one Charlie was still struggling to wrap his head around. Apparently, three years ago Lester had gotten his first job as a field reporter, fresh out of college. With a mass communications degree and no experience under his belt, he'd taken the position as a sign that he was going to be an anchor in no time. One day, he'd be a legend like Walter Cronkite or Peter Jennings.

But Channel 8 hadn't seen his potential, the way Lester told it. Not at first, anyway. They'd given him nothing but local fluff pieces about restaurant openings and animal shelters. He'd thought to himself that what he needed was a big story, something to show the higher-ups that he had chops. For that to work, he'd need to be out in the field when something went down. If he were first on the scene, he could scoop the story and broadcast live.

Unfortunately, the chances of that happening were astronomical.

That was when Lester had gotten an idea. He couldn't wait for fate to intervene, so he'd decided to create his own fate. It made sense, in a weird way. That was why he always set the fires during the day. It guaranteed the footage would be recapped during the evening news, when absolutely everyone would see it. Setting the fires in the middle of the night would mean most of the airplay happened while people were sleeping, and by the next morning, a small, easily managed fire would be old news.

Lester had never intended to hurt anyone. In fact, he'd never intended to become a serial criminal. He'd thought he'd set one small fire at a mall, "miraculously" happen to be at the scene, and the excitement of an emergency being broadcasted live from such a populous place would do the rest.

It hadn't been enough, though. He'd gotten some praise at work for his quick actions, but the fluff pieces had kept on coming. Lester had needed to up the ante. So, he'd become the serial arsonist. It'd taken four fires, but by the end of it, he'd been bumped up to real-reporter status.

Oh, but then, he'd gotten his real big break. The police brought in Billy Ray Phelan for questioning, and Peter managed to bribe a rookie cop into giving him the details. He'd released his video, and the rest was history. Once he'd gotten his fifteen minutes, he'd retired his firebug act, thinking it was all over.

Only now, years later, there was an anchor position open at Channel 8, and Lester wanted it *bad*. The choice had been between him and another reporter who'd just done an investigative piece on sex trafficking that'd made it into the *Times*. Calling the competition fierce would be an insult to competition.

So, Lester had busted out his arsonist act again. He always made sure the fires were small and easily contained. He wasn't a criminal at heart, just an ambitious man who'd gotten carried away.

Or so he'd claimed in the interrogation room. Charlie had told him to save it for a judge. No one could predict what a fire would do, and the locations he'd chosen were no joke. If Charlie had any say in the matter, Lester was going away for a long, long time.

"You finished with that report?"

Charlie glanced up from the papers in his hand. "Almost, sir."

Chief Bakay was what a Hollywood script would describe as "the proverbial police chief." A white, middle-aged man with a severe face and the smell of cigars clinging to his crisp blue suit. Charlie had been on the receiving end of more than one stern talking-to from him, but it was hard to complain about it. The chief was painstakingly fair.

When Charlie had failed to catch the arsonist the first time around, Chief Bakay had made his disappointment clear. But when the case had been reopened, he'd also agreed to make Charlie lead investigator, allowing him another shot.

"Take your time with it. We want everything done right." The chief surveyed the nearly empty precinct. Messy desks identical to Charlie's dotted the green carpet, washed out by the fluorescent overhead lights. "Don't want this bastard to walk after all the hours we put into catching him."

Charlie genuinely couldn't agree more. "Yes, sir."

When the chief looked back at him, a small smile crinkled his lined face. "I don't want to sound condescending—or worse, fatherly—but I'm proud of you. You didn't give up, and you got your man in the end."

Giddy emotion swelled in Charlie's chest. He was proud of himself as well. "Thank you."

"I just got off the phone with the mayor. He heard all about how you ran the suspect down on foot while a fire blazed in the background. The news channels are making you sound like James Bond. The mayor wants to give you a commendation for bravery."

"That's amazing. I'm honored." Charlie hesitated. "What about the firefighter who helped me? The one I mentioned in my initial report? The capture went much more smoothly thanks to him." All evening Charlie had been shaking off the memory of the potent kiss they'd shared in the parking lot.

Chief Bakay gave him an odd look. "I don't think the mayor would call me to commend someone who doesn't work for me."

Oh. Duh.

He continued. "But I imagine the firefighter will get a commendation as well. There's going to be a ceremony on Saturday. Make sure your formal uniform still fits. I don't think I've seen you wear it since you were a rookie fresh from the police academy."

The hint of teasing to his tone told Charlie the hidden meaning behind his words: Charlie had come a long way, and the difference was noticeable.

"I'll do that."

The chief bid him good night. Charlie stood as he left, watching until he was out the door. After, Charlie finally gave in and glanced at the clock. Cursing under his breath, he debated between triple-checking his report and calling it a night.

Unbidden, his thoughts drifted back to Eli. He remembered quite well how Eli felt about medals and hero labels. How was he going to react to this ceremony on Saturday? Would he be upset, or was he ready to accept the fact that he'd proven his bravery yet again?

Charlie desperately wanted to know, but that would mean facing Eli, and he wasn't certain *he* was ready for that. He was still furious at him, kiss or not. He doubted Eli had forgiven him either, for that matter. They needed to have a serious sit-down discussion.

Not tonight, though. Tonight, you need sleep. Well-earned sleep at that.

Good God, was he ever looking forward to getting into bed, relaxing, and knowing the arsonist was behind bars.

Or at least he was until he remembered Eli wouldn't be curled up next to him. Eli wouldn't be celebrating this victory with him.

With a sigh, Charlie clicked off his green lamp, grabbed his cell phone off the desk, and headed home, once more to an apartment that had been feeling emptier and emptier every day.

CHAPTER 11

The ceremony was a gorgeous affair. Having never been to one before, Eli was suitably impressed. A stage had been set up in a scenic park downtown. Red, white, and blue streamers decorated the trees, and spring flowers were in full bloom. A nearby fountain added the sound of splashing water to the breeze whistling through green leaves.

Eli showed up in his official uniform, which consisted of black dress pants and a double-breasted jacket with large gold buttons. His badge was pinned to his chest, and on his left arm was stitched the crest of the Louisville Fire Department. After fiddling with his black-and-white hat all morning, he'd finally gotten it to lie flat on his springy hair.

Chief Sappenfield had given him a basic idea of what to expect. Eli and several other members of the FD would receive thanks from the mayor, including the chief and Rogers, who'd worked on the arson case previously as well.

Eli wasn't *nervous* necessarily, but it was a good thing he couldn't argue with the mayor, or he might have tried to get out of this. It'd taken a lot of arguing with himself to get him accustomed to the idea that he was going to be honored, in public, for heroics in the field.

And even more so, he deserved it. It was time for him to accept that. Not that knowing made it any easier.

The weather was delightfully mild for the middle of the rainy season. Clear skies and a cool breeze greeted him as he strolled toward the stage. Other members of the FD gathered behind it in their sharp uniforms, along with others dressed in navy blue. Probably the police department.

His eyes snagged unerringly on someone he'd been futilely praying wouldn't be there: Charlie.

And *fuck*, he looked gorgeous.

Realistically, his uniform wasn't all that different from Eli's—a navy suit with a police crest on the arm and a shined silver badge on the chest—but he wore it so well. Standing with his shoulders back, his chin up, and a light smile playing across his lips, he seemed confident, and thrilled to be here.

That made sense. Charlie had caught the bad guy. He'd closed his case. Why wouldn't he be thrilled?

As if sensing Eli's gaze, Charlie glanced over. Eli wanted to flinch away, but forced himself to nod an acknowledgment. Charlie nodded back. When he turned around, the smile had been replaced with a serious expression.

Should I go over there? No. Now's really not the time to talk. We have roles to perform.

A crowd had gathered in front of the stage. Most were plopping down into the white folding chairs divided into two sections, but others stood at the back, mingling. Eli's dad was there, talking with Aunt Iola and her three kids.

More of Eli's family would be filing in soon. They'd all been thrilled when he'd called to tell them the news. Actually, the resounding reaction had been, "It's about damn time!" Hearing their excitement had done a lot to persuade him to accept this award.

Chief Sappenfield made her way over to him, looking especially official in her decorated uniform with medals on the breast and gold stripes on the sleeves. "You clean up well, Johnson."

"Same to you. I feel like I should salute you."

"A handshake will do fine."

They shook hands, both maintaining somber expressions for about three seconds. Then Chief Sappenfield laughed and tugged him into a brief hug. "Congratulations, Eli. You earned this."

The uncharacteristic display of affection hit Eli square. He wasn't the sort to get misty-eyed, but he had to clear his throat a few times before he could speak. "Thanks, Chief. Couldn't have done it without you."

She patted him on the back before glancing at the stage. "I think they're about to begin."

A quick peek in that direction confirmed it. The mayor had gotten up from a row of chairs placed next to a microphone. Ushers approached the people standing in the back and guided them to seats. A rustle of clothing and hushed voices fell over the assembly.

A few other officials were seated on the stage, all of whom had directed their attention to the mayor. Eli only recognized one of them—Assistant Chief Chilton, Sappenfield's superior—but there was one Eli would bet was Charlie's boss, the chief of police. He was wearing a special decorated uniform like Chief Sappenfield's, only in dark blue.

Charlie, who was only a few people down from Eli behind the stage, was watching Eli instead of the mayor.

The mayor stood in front of the microphone, index cards in hand and a bright politician's smile fixed on his face. "Thank you all for gathering here today to help me honor the brave individuals who worked tirelessly to rid our city of a dangerous criminal. Thanks to them, the Louisville arsonist has been apprehended."

Applause broke out, the loudest of which came from Eli's family, who'd snagged seats right up front. Their whoops of excitement made Eli relax for the first time since he'd arrived.

The mayor went on to deliver what was surely a moving speech, but Eli didn't hear a word. In his head, he was rehearsing over and over again what he'd have to do. He'd walk up onto stage, the mayor would pin a decorative bar onto his uniform, they'd shake hands, and then Eli would walk off the stage again *without* tripping all over himself. Or at least, he prayed he would.

Subtly, he slid a hand into his jacket and felt around for the breast pocket. When his fingers touched what they were groping for, an infusion of strength swept through him.

The mayor interrupted his fretting. "I'd like to welcome onto the stage Detective Charles Thorpe. He worked diligently on this case for three years, both as a rookie and as lead investigator. His courage and perseverance were instrumental to its success."

The audience applauded as Charlie took the stage. He looked so proud as he shook hands with the mayor, received his commendation, and waved at the crowd, beaming all the while. Watching him reminded Eli what had attracted him to Charlie in the first place, and it instilled new confidence in him.

Good thing too, because the mayor called his name next.

Eli focused on breathing as he walked onto the stage. The second he appeared, his family exploded into cheers. He kept walking, but a grin crawled onto his face no matter how hard he tried to appear neutral and dignified.

He made it all the way through the ritual in a stupor and was tripping down the stairs on the other side of the stage when emotions burst in his chest, as if a balloon had popped. He lowered his head and breathed through the sudden onslaught. The feelings were like a handful of tennis balls bouncing against his ribs, jabbing at him in quick succession, but he could identify anxiety and a whole lot of pride.

"You okay?"

Eli didn't need to glance up to know Charlie was standing next to him. Had he been waiting at the other end of the stage for him? Or did Eli seem like he was having some sort of breakdown? Probably both.

Wiping a hand down his face, Eli glanced at Charlie. "I'm fine. Just processing. Public appearances aren't my forte."

"Anything I can do to help?"

"No."

Awkward silence blanketed them.

Chewing on his bottom lip, Charlie seemed to hesitate. Eventually, he sighed. "You look so handsome in your uniform. I wish your mom could have been here to see you. I'm sure you wish the same thing."

Eli's heart fluttered. "She was here, in a way." He reached into his breast pocket and pulled out the picture he'd stowed there: the one from his fridge. He handed it to Charlie.

Charlie had barely glanced at it before his expression tightened with emotion. "You had her picture with you. God, right in the feels. I know you know this, but she would have been overjoyed to see you get this recognition." He passed the photo back.

Eli slipped it into his pocket and patted it through his jacket, above where his heart was. Feeling it beat spurred him to action. "Charlie— You do go by Charlie, right? Not Charles?"

Charlie's face reddened as he nodded.

"Right. I feel like there's something you're not saying. You must've come over here for a reason. What is it?"

Charlie shrugged, not quite meeting his eye. "I wasn't sure how you'd feel about all this. I know your stance on being called a hero. I've been wondering for days now if today was going to be a total nightmare for you."

"Thanks for the thought, but actually, I've had a change of heart about that."

Charlie's eyebrows shot up. "You have?"

"Well, not entirely. That'll take some time. But yeah, I've realized some things about my attitudes. I need to cut myself some slack and accept a little credit every now and then. Funnily enough, it was the arsonist who got me thinking."

"The *arsonist*?"

Eli nodded. "He was a guy who was so invested in his job, he lost sight of reality. I'm not saying what I was doing to myself was that extreme, but I was always pushing myself to do better, to do good, and never letting myself take any credit for my achievements. I was probably headed for a breakdown myself. Somewhere along the way I lost sight of the real goal: leave the world a better place than it was before. I let my mom's message get warped. Accepting this commendation today was the first step to getting back on the right path."

"Huh." Charlie shuffled his feet. "I suppose I can see that. It's a lesson I need to learn as well."

Eli considered him before speaking. "For the record, you were a part of my revelation too."

"I was?"

"You were the first person who ever called me a hero that made me want to be one."

Charlie was quiet for a long moment. "What are you doing with the rest of your Saturday?"

"Talking to you."

Charlie let out a bark of laughter. "Did you drive here?"

"Yeah."

"Give me a second to tell my mom I found a ride, and then can we go to your place? I miss your cats. I hate that I didn't get to say goodbye to them."

Eli hesitated, not because he didn't want to talk to Charlie, but because he really, really did. Was going to a place with privacy and a bedroom a good idea? "I don't want to take you away from your family. I'm sure they want to congratulate you."

"It's just my parents. I don't have a whole cheerleading section like you do. I'd invite you to meet them, but . . ." He pursed his lips. "If that's going to happen, I want it to be when there's no weirdness between us."

It was Eli's turn to get hot in the face. "I'll wait for you right here."

"Back in a sec."

It was impossible not to watch him go, but considering the circumstances, Eli hedged his more perverted thoughts. That was, until Charlie looked back at him. At first, his face was blank. Then he offered Eli a small, brilliant smile.

For the first time since Charlie had ordered Eli out of his apartment, Eli dared to hope.

The second Charlie walked into Eli's kitchen, he heard small feet bounding toward him. Pistol, Moxie, and Chutzpah all shot into the room at once, a blur of fur and a cacophony of insistent meows.

He dropped to his knees and held his arms out. "Kitties! I missed y'all so much."

Pistol got directly into his lap and flopped, not caring that he slid down Charlie's thighs to the floor. Moxie hopped up on two legs and put her paws on his arm while Chutzpah circled him like a shark, meowing his head off.

"Oh, I see how it is." Eli closed the door behind them. "Can't remember the last time I got home and was greeted with anything other than demands for dinner."

At the word *dinner*, Chutzpah and Moxie immediately lost interest in Charlie and started rubbing up against Eli's ankles. Pistol remained firmly pooled at Charlie's knees like a pile of plushy soot.

Charlie gave the black cat a thorough under-chin scratching. "Now I know who really loves me."

"They all love you, but they also love food." Eli dropped his hat onto the table, put his mom's photograph back onto the fridge, and inched around them so he could get to the container of dry food under the sink. He filled a big mason jar and dumped it into three bowls. At the sound of kibble, Pistol finally succumbed to temptation. He rolled to his feet and waddled over to his dish.

Charlie chuckled. "They say this is a fraction of what it's like to have kids."

"Yeah. Maybe we'll get to compare someday." Eli was leaning against the sink, but at that, he straightened up. "By 'we,' I don't mean—"

Charlie waved him off before climbing to his feet. "I knew what you meant." He took his hat off as well and tossed it next to Eli's. It was odd how similar they looked, and yet the metal crests in the center were totally different.

Eli blew out a breath that whistled through his teeth. "You want a beer or something?"

"No, thanks."

Quiet descended on them again. There was so much Charlie wanted to say, he couldn't think of where to start. Eli seemed to be having the same problem.

Eventually, Charlie's subtlety ran thin. "I'm still angry at you."

"I'm still mad at you too."

"Good."

Eli raised an eyebrow at him.

"If you weren't, it would mean you didn't take this seriously," Charlie explained.

"Ah." Eli leaned back, palms flat on the counter. His musculature was visible through the layers of his uniform, especially his biceps stretching the sleeves.

Charlie tore his eyes away. "I will say one thing, though. I was happy to see you at the ceremony."

"Because you missed me, or because you thought I wasn't going to show?"

"A bit of both. I won't deny that it's been strange sleeping in an empty bed this past week. Has it been for you?"

Eli smiled sadly. "Of course."

Charlie wet his lips, thinking about his next words. "This is going to sound odd, but you being there today meant a lot to me."

"Why?"

"I think it shows that you've changed. Grown. Before, I think you would have turned the mayor down or maybe asked the chief to go in your place. But today, you stood up in front of everyone and accepted what you deserved. By doing that, to me, you were acknowledging that you can be wrong. In a good way."

Eli pushed off the counter and took a step toward him. "I can be wrong in bad ways too. Charlie, I'm so sorry. I never should have accused you of what I did. I lost my head. I never meant to hurt you."

Charlie exhaled audibly. "You didn't mean to, but you did anyway."

"Yeah," Eli said, looking miserable. "I did."

There was a beat of silence before Charlie nodded. "Thank you for acknowledging it. I hurt you too, every time I lied to you. I knew I was digging myself a hole, but the job was so important to me. I had the opposite problem from you: I thought I had something to prove. I would have done anything to get this medal that's pinned to my chest right now."

"You were never a failure, Charlie." Eli's voice was rough with emotion. "I hope you realize that now."

Charlie nodded. "I understood what you meant when you said that thing about messages getting warped along the way. Especially when you think you're doing what's right. After this case, I asked Chief Bakay not to assign me any more undercover work. Having that other identity—Charlie Kinnear—made me act in ways I normally wouldn't. Some of those ways were good, like when I asked you out, but obviously others weren't. I lost sight of who I am and what's important to me." He paused. "And *who* is important."

Eli let out a shuddering breath. "I know what you mean."

"It's funny, you and I are so similar, but we make such different choices."

Eli took another step closer. "I think we are too." He was looking down, eyelashes dark over his brown eyes. "Can you forgive me? Maybe not today, but someday?"

Charlie's pulse started to race. "In time, provided you *never* do that to me again. Unless, you know, I show up on your doorstep with a severed head or something. Then you can make all the accusations you want."

Genuine laughter poured from Eli, rich and deep. He glanced up, eye sparkling. "I think I can handle that."

"Do you forgive me? For lying to you?"

Eli's mirth dampened a bit, but he nodded. He reached out and squeezed Charlie's waist affectionately. "I do. I know you thought you didn't have a choice and that there was a lot resting on this. For the record, I would have kept your secret, though."

"As time passed, part of me knew that. I was overzealous." Now Charlie's heart was racing in earnest. He moved closer, and heat immediately sprang up between them. "So, we're okay? Or do I need to butter you up some more?"

It felt so natural, flirting with Eli again. Things weren't perfect between them, but it was like they were magnets, being tugged toward each other no matter how much they resisted. Charlie didn't want to fight it anymore. He wanted to fall into Eli's arms and stay there.

"I think we're more than okay." Eli's hand was still on his waist. "I've missed you. It didn't help that—" He looked away.

Charlie touched his chin and lightly turned his face back. "What?"

"There was never a moment when I stopped wanting you. At the height of my anger, I still wanted every part of you."

A dizzy spell swept over Charlie, in a good way. "Same. My feelings never changed." He fingered one of the gold buttons on Eli's jacket lightly with his index finger. "I meant it when I said your uniform looks incredible on you. I like you in your turnout gear, but this is better."

Laughter rumbled in Eli's chest. "I wanted to return the compliment earlier. After seeing you in street clothes this whole time, the uniform was a treat. I love this color on you." He trailed a hand up Charlie's torso.

Charlie had to struggle to keep his breathing even. "I wasn't always in street clothes."

Eli blinked, and then as understanding visibly dawned on him, his eyes smoldered.

Stepping closer until they were inches apart, Charlie searched his eyes. "Which do you prefer? Dressed up or down?"

"How dressed down are we talking?" Eli licked his lips. "And is both an option?"

"You tell me."

The hand on Charlie's waist slid to the bottom button on his uniform. With just his thumb and index finger, Eli popped it open. Charlie found himself leaning back against the counter so he could watch Eli's fingers slipping up his front, undoing buttons as they went.

When he had Charlie's jacket open, he flattened his palm over Charlie's stomach, above his pants. His fingers flexed, and the strength in them made Charlie woozy. Eli dragged his hand up, bringing Charlie's white dress shirt with it. He brushed the pad of his thumb against Charlie's tattoo.

Charlie's head fell back and hit a cabinet with a soft *thunk*. "That shouldn't feel so good."

"You shouldn't *look* so good." Eli stepped between his spread legs, and suddenly the kitchen was ten degrees hotter. He pressed a kiss to Charlie's jaw. "Half-undressed like this, caught between proper and debauched. You look *filthy*."

Charlie groaned and turned his head for a real kiss. Eli gave it to him, slow and deep. He dipped his tongue into Charlie's partially open mouth, and God, it was wonderful to taste him again. Eli pressed him to the counter using only his hips. Charlie bucked against him, already getting hard and praying this was going where he thought it was.

Eli must've been thinking the same thing, because he broke the kiss long enough to pant, "Is this okay? Am I going too fast?"

Charlie almost laughed. "Honestly, you could speed things up. After a whole week without you, I'm horny as fuck. Missed this. Missed you." He rolled his hips again to emphasize the point, his dick nudging up against Eli's muscular thigh.

Eli shuddered beautifully. "I don't want to sleep with you if you're still mad at me, though. This isn't scratching an itch for me. You must know that by now."

Charlie wrangled in his libido long enough to wrap his arms around Eli, hold him close, and press his mouth to Eli's ear. "It's not that for me either. There was something I wanted to say to you before all this mess went down. I'm not going to say it now because we're still in a weird place, but . . . will you let me show you?"

Eli huffed a laugh that had an edge of emotion to it and nodded. "Yes."

Charlie grabbed hold of Eli's lapels and hauled him in for a bruising kiss. Eli groaned against his lips and planted his palms on the counter behind Charlie, caging him in. Everything became a blur of skin and hands as they both moved to shove clothing out of the way, never breaking their kiss.

Charlie was in the process of ripping Eli's pants open when Eli grabbed him—almost picking him up—and spun him around to another stretch of the counter, one that was blissfully free of cabinets and appliances.

He maneuvered Charlie so he was facing the counter, leaning on it with his ass stuck out. Eli ground against him, so hard Charlie could feel him distinctly through their pants.

"Want you so bad." Eli traced the shell of Charlie's ear with his tongue. "Can I have you?"

Charlie was so turned on, he couldn't find the breath to respond. He nodded and wrapped a hand around the back of Eli's neck, turning his head so their mouths could meet. He couldn't see what happened next, but he heard fumbling, a low rumble of pleasure from Eli, and then his own pants were being shoved down to his thighs.

"We can't mess up our uniforms," Charlie gasped, doing absolutely nothing to stop Eli.

Eli licked his throat. "We'll have them cleaned."

"What about the cats?"

"Like anything could distract them from food." Eli nipped at his ear. "Bend over."

Charlie scrambled to comply, resting on his elbows. "Condom?"

"Way ahead of you." Eli opened a drawer to his left and produced one like a magic trick.

Charlie couldn't help but laugh. "You keep condoms in your kitchen?"

Eli bit the back of his neck. "You complaining?"

A moan was all Charlie could say in response. There wasn't lube, but between spit and Charlie's all-encompassing desire to get fucked, they made it work. A few minutes later, Eli was rolling the condom on, and Charlie was bracing one hand against the wall.

He expected to feel the head of Eli's cock, but instead, Eli pushed Charlie's jacket and shirt—still mostly on—up his back and then stilled.

"Problem?" Charlie asked, out of breath.

"No, it's just . . ." Eli leaned down and kissed his nape. "You don't know how *good* you look. Clothes all mussed, bent over with your pants around your knees. I've never had a thing for uniforms, but you in this prim outfit, all debauched . . . I'm savoring the view."

Impatient, Charlie pressed his ass back against him. "I know a much better way you can savor me."

That seemed to break through to Eli. He made a little hungry sound and finally sunk into Charlie. It wasn't a totally smooth motion, thanks to the quick preparation, but Charlie was treated to the pure, nerve-tingling sensation of being filled. He grunted in little bursts with every inch, until Eli was in him as far as he could go.

Nuzzling the back of Charlie's neck, Eli held himself still. "How does it—"

Charlie placed both hands flat on the counter and growled, "*Move.*"

Eli's pace was slow at first, but it took no time to build. He must've been remembering what it was like to fuck Charlie, how hard he could go, what limits he could push. Charlie tried to keep a hold of himself, but Eli had him crying out within minutes. Dishes rattled in the cabinets connected to the counter, but he didn't care. The whole house could come down around them, and he doubted he'd notice, it felt so good.

Eli, for his part, was cursing freely, sounding so broken it made Charlie giddy. His voice wavered every time he thrust hard into Charlie, the only sign that he was losing it. His rhythm remained steady and brutal. Charlie was questioning if he'd even need to touch himself to get off when Eli pressed his chest to Charlie's back, wrapped an arm around him, and reached for his cock.

"Close," Eli gasped. "Almost there." He stroked Charlie's wet cock with trembling fingers.

"F-feels so good," Charlie stammered back. There was a thought that'd been forming in his head all the while, and he finally managed to get his tongue around it. "After all the times we've fucked, why does it feel so much better now?"

Eli squeezed the arm around Charlie's chest like he wished he could somehow pull him closer. "You know why. You must know—Charlie, I—"

Charlie heard the words Eli was trying to say loud and clear. Not in his head, but in his heart.

I love you.

Charlie came *explosively*. It almost hurt, he came so hard. It was a good thing he was leaning on the counter, because his knees buckled. Eli held him up while thrusting into him a handful more times, and then Eli grunted through what sounded like an earth-shattering orgasm of his own.

Thankfully, Eli managed to keep both of them on their feet as they breathed through the aftershocks. Charlie was sweaty, limp, and dazed as pleasure plucked a few final chords in his belly before fading, leaving an afterimage of the intensity.

A long moment passed before he gathered himself enough to prop himself onto his elbows. "Holy shit."

Eli nodded, his nose rubbing the back of Charlie's neck. "I think my knees locked."

"I'll take that as a compliment, though you're crushing me a little."

Eli chuckled and kissed his sweaty skin. "Sorry, *muffin*." He released his arm from around Charlie, pushed himself upright, and pulled out of him with a hiss.

Charlie missed Eli the second he moved away, no matter how happy his muscles were. A sudden lack of warmth behind him and some shuffling told him Eli was probably cleaning up. Charlie should do the same, assuming he found the ability to move sometime in the next year.

He glanced down at himself and cursed. His uniform was a hot mess. "Well, I guess I can't get another commendation anytime soon."

Warmth returned to his back as Eli wrapped him in a gentle hug. "Give me fifteen minutes, and I'll give you one myself."

Laughing, Charlie allowed himself to be hauled up and semicarried to Eli's bedroom, where he was deposited on the bed. Once there, Eli stripped off Charlie's shoes and took all the parts of his uniform that'd gotten messy.

"I'm just going to spot-check them so no stains set," he explained, kneeling next to the bed as he folded Charlie's pants. "We'll take them to a dry cleaner later."

"You're amazing." He said it with a laugh, but it was true. "I can't *move*, and you're doing laundry."

"Well, it's sort of my fault. It was worth it, though." He kissed Charlie before rising to his feet. "We might be getting this uniform dry-cleaned a lot in the future, because we're definitely doing *that* again."

He exited the room. Charlie wasn't sure how much time passed, hormone-addled as he was, but when Eli returned, he'd stripped down to boxers and an undershirt. It was unfair how sexy he looked in such simple clothing.

Eli climbed into bed and lay down next to Charlie. "How are you?"

Charlie snuggled up to him, sliding an arm over his waist. "Much better now that I'm here. I missed this bed. I missed you."

Pistol appeared at the foot of the mattress as if summoned by Charlie's sentiment. He padded up to them, and—after several futile attempts to insert himself between them—flopped down against Charlie's back.

"He loves you." Eli chuckled. His face sobered. "He's not the only one."

There was so much Charlie wanted to say, it felt like the words were fighting with each other in his skull. He'd intended to have this conversation later, when things had gone back to normal, and they'd had a few more talks about trust and forgiveness.

But now that he was nestled up in bed with Eli, warm and happy, he felt like for the first time in a week, he was precisely where he was supposed to be. Everything was right.

"Eli, I didn't love you when I first met you," Charlie said, choosing his words carefully. "It wasn't love at first sight. The sky didn't light up with fireworks, and music didn't crescendo in the background. But when I talked to you, I knew something special was happening. That's why I didn't give up at first. I'm sorry I almost gave up later, because the truth is, after everything we've been through, I'm so in love with you now."

Eli's face tightened with emotion, and for a second, Charlie thought he'd fucked up, but then Eli grabbed his chin and kissed him. It bruised Charlie's lips, but he didn't care.

Pulling away enough to speak, Eli murmured, "You know I feel the same, right? Ever since you came into my life, it's been like I'm awake for the first time in months."

Charlie's eyelids were drooping. All the emotion of the past day—hell, the past week—had drained him. He managed to nod. "It's been the same for me. There are still some things I want to talk about, but if you're in this, I am too."

"I am." Eli kissed him again, gently. A featherlight brush of lips. "Besides, if you stopped coming around, I don't think Pistol would ever forgive me. I'd wake up to mouse heads in my bed."

Maybe Charlie was a little drunk on happiness, because for some reason, that was the funniest thing he'd ever heard. He burst into giggles and was quickly joined by Eli. The noise woke a dozing Pistol, who added his yowling to the mix, somehow making it funnier.

It was in that moment, while Charlie lay in a sun-warmed bed sandwiched by two beings who loved him, that his priorities finally fell into place, and he knew he'd found what he really wanted.

EPILOGUE

Six Months Later

Eli stood on the front lawn—*his* front lawn; he still couldn't believe it—and gazed up at the freshly painted cottage before him, a smile tugging at his lips.

Three whole days after moving in, it was still strange to wake up in a new bedroom, go to work, and then drive to this cute little house he could now call home.

What was even better, however, was the other car waiting for him in the driveway.

"Happy housewarming, love." Charlie appeared at his side with two glasses of champagne, one of which he handed to Eli. "What are you thinking about?"

"Oh, nothing." Eli tapped the flute against Charlie's, making a dainty, bell-like sound. "Just that for once in my life, I can't think of anything that could make me happier."

"I know exactly what you mean." Charlie sipped his champagne before twining their fingers together. "Our first house. I know it's a rental, but it really feels like it's ours, doesn't it?"

"Yeah, it's a perfect starter. Plenty of space. Even the cats are happy." He squeezed Charlie's hand. "And, you know, living with you isn't half-bad either."

"Like we didn't practically live together before."

"True, but I've enjoyed making it official."

"Same." Charlie pecked his cheek. "My sister wants to come by with the kids and see it."

"Tell her she's welcome anytime. Lord knows my dad's already asked if there's a guest room for him."

They stood together on the crisp green grass—fingers intertwined and shoulders touching—for a moment longer before Charlie turned to face him. "I have a surprise for you. I set it up while you were at work, with a little help."

"What is it?"

"Do you trust me?"

Eli didn't hesitate. "Completely."

Charlie took their glasses and set them on the roof of Eli's car. Then, he pulled a blue tie out of his back pocket. "I'm going to cover your eyes. No peeking, okay?"

"Okay."

Charlie tied the silky fabric loosely around his eyes. It was disorienting for a moment, but then Charlie took both his hands. "I'm going to guide you. We're not going far."

Excitement built in Eli as they started to walk. He tried to guess what Charlie was up to, but honestly, the man was full of surprises. Eli had learned that the very first day they'd met.

It was hard to judge distance with his eyes covered, but Eli figured that Charlie was leading him around back. His suspicions were confirmed when Charlie let go of his hands, and Eli heard the squeak of the metal gate leading into the backyard—a *real* backyard, with a fence and everything.

Hushed voices reached his ears along with a high-pitched sound he didn't recognize. He couldn't be certain, but he thought he heard Charlie shush someone.

"Charlie?"

"I'm here, love." Charlie took his hands again. "Don't look yet. We're almost there."

Mulch crunched under Eli's feet (the rose bed next to the gate), followed by what he guessed was stone (the path leading from the shed to the back door), and then grass again.

Eli's excitement was quickly turning into amusement as he pictured all sorts of scenarios: an over-the-top backyard picnic, or knowing Charlie, he'd gotten them something ridiculous like a Slip 'N Slide.

"Babe, can I look yet? I—"

And that was when Eli heard it. The high-pitched noise from before transformed into a distinct whine. One he recognized from movies, and the park, and all the times he'd taken the cats to the vet.

He sucked in a breath. "Is that . . ."

"All right, love." Charlie untied the fabric covering his eyes. "Look."

Eli opened them. Anette and Chief Sappenfield were kneeling on the grass. Anette had a huge grin on her face, and Chief Sappenfield was looking relaxed for once in civilian clothing.

But most importantly, they were both crouching in front of a wooden dog house that definitely hadn't been there yesterday, holding the red collar of a young dalmatian.

"Surprise!" they called at the same time.

Anette, who'd been holding a treat in front of the dalmatian's nose, presumably to distract them, let it drop. The dog snapped it up and then barked enthusiastically.

"Oh my *God*." Eli rushed over to the dog, who wriggled with sheer joy. "You got me a *dog*?"

Charlie's whole face was pure glee. "When I went to pick up the cats' meds from the pet hospital, I took a stroll through their shelter. There she was, right up front. I swear, it was like a sign. You always said you wanted a dog as soon as you had a yard, and what better breed for a firefighter?"

"She's *beautiful*." Eli tried to pet her, but she was too busy licking his hand and rubbing up against his legs. "And energetic." He glanced at his friends. "I suspect you two were in charge of keeping her from rushing us the second we appeared."

"It was our pleasure," Chief Sappenfield said, favoring him with a rare bright smile. "Charlie called yesterday to enlist our help. I'm surprised you weren't suspicious when both of us left work early."

"I didn't think twice about it, honestly. Thank you both." He gave each of them a hug before turning to Charlie. "What's her name?"

"They were calling her Sherise down at the shelter, but I think we can do better than that." Charlie paused, seemingly in thought. "We could name her after your mom."

Eli shook his head. "She wasn't a dog person. She wouldn't have liked that."

"All right. Any ideas?"

Eli grinned. "Spot." The sheer affront that earned him made Eli burst out laughing. "Well, what do you suggest?"

"You know me, love." Next to him, Charlie bent down to pet the dog, who seemed doubly excited to have two sets of hands on her now. "I'd probably make a bad joke. Nothing as trite as Spot, but something else."

"Like what?"

Charlie thought for a second. "Well, she has a red collar. That makes her black and white and red all over."

Anette chuckled. "You can't name a dog Newspaper. What would you call her for short? Noose?"

"What about something that means newspaper?" Chief Sappenfield suggested.

"I like that." Charlie tapped his chin. "My first instinct is to call her Extra, because she certainly has a lot of extra energy, but that's a terrible name. What about Daily?"

"I love it." Eli crouched down and took Daily's sweet face in his hands. "What do you think, Daily the Dalmatian?"

She licked the tip of his nose, which was a good enough response for him.

Anette sighed dreamily. "What a perfect little family."

"It does have a certain poetry to it," Charlie said. "Very domestic. It reminds me of something you said when we first met."

Eli stood up again, prompting Daily to sit practically on top of his feet. "What?"

"You had these goals for what you wanted out of life. Remember?"

"Oh yeah." Eli grinned, realizing where this was going. "I had a whole list. Now that you mention it, I've checked a lot of them off. A successful career."

"Check," Chief Sappenfield said with a wink.

"A house with a yard."

"Check," Anette chirped.

Charlie added, "And now the dog. That's almost everything. All that's missing is . . ."

Eli touched his chin, drawing him closer. "Marriage to the man of my dreams."

A blush crept over Charlie's face that was so damn cute, Eli kissed both of his hot cheeks.

Anette pumped a fist in the air. "Groomsmaid, here I come!"

Chief Sappenfield joked about having the wedding at the station, and Charlie suggested they slide down the pole instead of walking down the aisle. That image made Eli laugh so hard he was nearly in tears.

While the others bantered—Daily barking as if contributing to the conversation—Eli took Charlie's hand and squeezed, thinking to himself that he hadn't known it was possible to be this happy.

Dear Reader,

Thank you for reading Avery Giles's *Too Hot*!

We know your time is precious and you have many, many entertainment options, so it means a lot that you've chosen to spend your time reading. We really hope you enjoyed it.

We'd be honored if you'd consider posting a review—good or bad—on sites like **Amazon, Barnes & Noble, Kobo, Goodreads, Twitter, Facebook, Tumblr,** and your blog or website. We'd also be honored if you told your friends and family about this book. Word of mouth is a book's lifeblood!

For more information on upcoming releases, author interviews, blog tours, contests, giveaways, and more, please sign up for our weekly, spam-free newsletter and visit us around the web:

Newsletter: riptidepublishing.com/newsletter
Twitter: twitter.com/RiptideBooks
Facebook: facebook.com/RiptidePublishing
Goodreads: tinyurl.com/RiptideOnGoodreads
Tumblr: riptidepublishing.tumblr.com

Thank you so much for Reading the Rainbow!

RiptidePublishing.com

ABOUT THE AUTHOR

Avery Giles is a brown-eyed, fair-haired, moss-covered swamp witch who subsists on energy drinks and the hearts of her enemies. Her day-to-day routine involves waking up, writing three sentences, staring at those three sentences until her brain tells her why they're wrong, watching eighteen hours of Netflix, and luring bandits away from the safety of the well-lit path. If asked about her favorite books, she'll mention the Percy Jackson series, *Good Omens*, and the blackened scroll on which she detailed an encounter with a crooked librarian that led to two marriages and a beheading. She enjoys eating Italian, French, and German lovers after mating with them.

Connect with Avery:

email: authoraverygiles@gmail.com

Enjoy more stories like
Too Hot!
at RiptidePublishing.com!

Get a Grip

The Secret of Hunter's Bog

If a tree falls in Bluewater Bay . . .
could it be fate?

With their lives on the line, their
only way to safety is together.

ISBN: 978-1-62649-608-8

ISBN: 978-1-62649-374-2

CPSIA information can be obtained
at www.ICGtesting.com
Printed in the USA
LVHW111805080119
603164LV00005B/726/P

9 781626 498600